The Proof of the I

A Bartlett and Boase Mystery

Marina Pascoe

Copyright © 2018 Marina Pascoe

Published by Morvoren Press

All rights reserved, including the right to reproduce this book, or portions thereof in any form. No part of this text may be reproduced, transmitted, downloaded, decompiled, reverse engineered, or stored, in any form or introduced into any information storage and retrieval system, in any form or by any means, whether electronic or mechanical without the express written permission of the author.

This is a work of fiction. Names and characters are the product of the author's imagination and any resemblance to actual persons, living or dead, is entirely coincidental.

The views expressed in this work are solely those of the author and do not necessarily reflect the views of the publisher, and the publisher hereby disclaims any responsibility for them.

ISBN: 978-0-244-67928-6

Other books in the series
Empty Vessels
Too Many Cooks
A Fool and His Money

To find out more about the world of Bartlett and Boase – or to contact Marina Pascoe, go to:
https://www.marinapascoe.com/

Chapter One

'Oh, do come in please. This is ever so kind of you – you know, to help me out like this. I've been sick with worry ever since I found out.'

Marjorie Medlin held open the scullery door to allow the woman to pass through. She carried on talking while the woman removed her coat and laid it across the back of a kitchen chair. A girl of about ten was sitting at a small table with a younger girl of around six sitting on her knee. On the floor a small boy, and the youngest of the three children, played with a tin train. He pulled at the woman's hem. She looked down at him and then at the woman.

'Well now, dear, I can quite see the predicament you're in.'

'Yes. They can't go to school today – they've had the measles and they're not allowed back in until Monday. It's so hard to occupy them when they're home all day. I've just been listening to Tommy Boyce with the golden voice. Harold bought us a new wireless set for Christmas – he'd been saving for ages. It's ever so good. Have you got one? A wireless?'

The woman replied, not looking up from rummaging in her coat pockets.

'No, dear. I haven't got a wireless. However, I was sure I had a handkerchief here somewhere. Ah, yes, there it is. Now dear, shall we go upstairs? Make haste please.'

Marjorie obliged and the woman followed her up to a neat front bedroom which contained a double bed, an oak chest of drawers, a wardrobe and a matching dressing table. Two dressing gowns hung on the back of the door. The woman went across to the window and peering out onto the other houses which made up Well Lane, pulled the curtains almost shut, all save a narrow gap which allowed the morning sunlight to filter through.

'Not expecting any callers are you?'

'No. No one. My husband won't be back until six. It will be all right, won't it?'

'Yes. It'll be all right. Now you just lay on the bed and make yourself comfortable. There's nothing to worry about. Try to relax and we'll be finished before you know. Just lift your skirt up above your waist for me.'

'Shall I take off my stockings?'

'No dear. No need. That's right. Good girl. You just relax.'

Archie Boase ran his fingers through his hair and sighed. Pulling open the top drawer of his desk, he reached to the back and pulled out a paper bag. He opened it carefully and pushed his nose inside. He sniffed. And sniffed again. No. He wouldn't risk it. There wasn't much that Boase wouldn't take a chance on when it came to food but this, well…he thought to himself for a moment. His landlady, Mrs Curgenven, gave him this sausage roll on…now, when was it? Tuesday. Yes, that was it. Tuesday. He was going for a walk and she thought he would like to take it with him in case he became hungry. Tuesday. Today was Monday and the Falmouth police station had been uncommonly warm this past week. He peered longingly into the bag and sniffed again. Well, he was rather hungry. No. He rolled up the bag and launched it into the air. It landed fortuitously in the waste basket next to Inspector George Bartlett's desk. Boase surveyed the empty desk opposite him and wondered how his old boss was getting along.

No one had been happy about the way George Bartlett had been removed from the station, indeed, from the force. Now alone and missing his older companion, whom Boase felt had taught him everything he knew about policing, the constable was feeling an emptiness in his life like he had never felt before. He didn't believe that was entirely due to the upset at work. No. The pain he was suffering went much deeper than that. Four months since he had parted from the love of his life, Irene Bartlett. He had been such a fool. And now, well now he spent his spare time wandering the streets of Falmouth, sitting on the beaches thinking about his girl and hoping to catch a glimpse of her. If he couldn't have Irene for his own then he would have no one. His landlady in whom he had confided, had told him he was still a young man – that there were still plenty of fish in the sea. How he hated that expression.

Boase opened up the second drawer in his desk and withdrew several scraps of paper. All messages in the desk sergeant's familiar scrawl and all saying the same – *'please call Mr Bartlett. Mr Bartlett would like to see you. Call in to the Bartlett's.'* These were going back some time and Boase had ignored them. He wanted more than anything to see Irene. But yet he didn't. What would he say? What if she had another beau? Boase pushed the notes back into the drawer and slammed it shut as hard as he could, tears pricking his eyes. What a fool he'd been. What a fool he still was!

As Boase thought about starting his day, the door opened and Constable Ernest Penhaligon leaned in.

'Sorry to bother you, Archie, only there's a woman outside says she wants to speak to you. I tried to tell her you were busy but she's very insistent.'

'Okay – I'll come out. Thanks Ernie.'

Boase left the office and crossed the lobby to the large leather bench seat next to the sergeant's desk. A woman in, Boase guessed her late fifties, was sitting there holding in her hand what looked like a piece of crumpled newspaper. As Boase approached her, she stood up.

'Good morning, Madam. I'm Constable Boase – how can I help you?'

'Good morning, Constable. My name is Dorothy Laity and I'd very much like you to look at this fish.'

The woman held open the newspaper and offered it up to Boase who, caught unawares by the smell as the newspaper unfolded, took a step back.

'Madam. I don't understand what you're asking me to do. I'm sorry.'

'Constable, it's very simple – I want you to look at this fish. It's a piece of 'addock.'

'But I don't understand what it has to do with me.'

'Constable – are you being deliberately difficult?'

Boase looked over his shoulder as he heard a loud snort coming from behind the sergeant's desk. He glared at Penhaligon. The woman persisted.

'Yes – and you over there, young man. You needn't laugh – my 'usband could 'ave died. Look, we was in George's Café two weeks ago – me an' me 'usband. We was 'avin' something to eat. I only 'ad a sandwich – see, I wasn't very 'ungry, but Percy, well Perce said 'e fancied a bit of sausage – 'e does like a nice sausage, Constable.'

Boase was now trying to take this seriously, his best efforts being hampered by the chuckles coming from both Penhaligon and now the desk sergeant who had just appeared.

'And, Madam...you consider this to be police business – I am very busy, I'm sure you understand.'

'Well, if you be a bit patient, I'm coming to that. That very night, Perce was ever so ill...up all night 'e was. Dot, 'e says, Dot, I do believe I've bin poisoned. Don't be daft, I said. They was probably just not very good sausages. Anyway, two days later 'e was much better and back down the docks. I went back and told the manageress. Told 'er straight I did – they sausages must 'ave bin off. There was 'ell up. So, she gave us a coupon for two free dinners – which I thought to meself, thas all right, and I forgot about it all. Yesterday, lo an' be'old – we went back. I 'ad a nice bit o' roast chicken – ansum twas and Perc 'ad this fish. Guess what?'

Boase stared, giving a good impression of someone who was trying to guess.

'No. What?'

'Perce was up all night again - same as before. This is what 'e 'ad. She thrust forward the newspaper again towards Boase.

'Now, Constable. Don't you think this is a bit fishy?'

Boase continued to stare at the woman, unable now to ignore the uncontrolled laughter coming from behind the sergeant's desk.

'Madam – I don't see...'

'Well. It's obvious innit? Someone's trying to poison me 'usband. What are you going goin' to do about it?'

'Madam, that's a very serious accusation you're making. Why would anyone want to poison your husband – and why in George's Café?'

'Well – you're the police...isn't that your job?'

'But, Madam – if your husband ate the fish then how come it's here now?'

'Well, 'e 'ad a few mouthfuls and then said it didn't taste right. So, being naturally suspicious after what 'appened in there before, I took the fish and put it in me 'andbag. Perce I

5

said, I'm takin' this to the police – I'm not 'appy about this and so we left.'

'Right.'

Boase was not in the mood for this just now.

'Let me know when you've found out what's goin' on. I've already left me details at the desk. Good day.'

At that, the woman, glaring at Boase, thrust the bundle of newspaper into his hands and left the station. Boase sat on the bench. What on earth was that about?

The day continued uneventfully for Boase. He felt a little isolated if he was honest – what with his friend and mentor, Inspector George Bartlett having left. Superintendent Bolton had said that Boase was to continue alone as best he could until a replacement came and under Bolton's supervision. To his credit, Boase had complied – and coped admirably. But now, well, it had been a few months and it was becoming a little wearing now. He supposed he should visit his old boss – he knew he would be more than welcome but, what of Irene? Truth be told, Boase was frightened. Yes, that was it. Archibald Boase was scared – of what might happen if he bumped into Irene. And yet, six months ago they had been so happy, making wedding plans and so in love. He missed her smile, missed the scent of lilacs in her hair, missed the way her nose wrinkled when she laughed. He missed her.

'Come on, Rabone – I'll buy you a cuppa at George's. You're about due to knock off? I ought to at least go there so I can tell that awful woman that I've investigated her fish.'

Boase and Constable Rabone took the walk from the police station, across the Moor and headed to Arwenack Street to the always popular George's Café. When they arrived the place seemed unusually quiet and they went up the stairs and found a table by the window overlooking the harbour.

'I never tire of that view, Rabone.'

'Nor me. I was born just over there…'

'Really? Where?'

'Flushing. My parents still live there.'

'I thought you were born here in Falmouth. I like Flushing. Yes, I like it a lot. Irene and I used to…'

Boase stopped himself and remained quiet while images of taking the boat across the river for a picnic with his girl flashed across his mind. A waitress came to the table, notepad and pencil in hand.

'Two teas please, Miss. Fancy a cake, Rabone?'

'Well, I'm a bit peckish – but I think I'll have a sandwich actually.'

'Me too – what sandwiches do you have, Miss?'

The waitress flipped her book over to the back page and read out the available options.

'We've got ham, cheese, fish paste, beef or chicken.'

Boase couldn't decide.

'I don't know – what are you having, Rabone?'

'I think I'll have the chicken.'

'Make that two please, Miss.'

Boase was happy not to have to think about anything. Just lately he had become such a ditherer – so unlike him, so out of character. The waitress returned promptly, cups and saucers rattling on the tray. She set down a large pot of tea with milk and sugar.

'Sandwiches won't be long.'

'She's quite a cutie, Archie.'

'Well, if you hadn't noticed, Ernie, she's wearing a ring.'

'So you were looking too?'

Boase turned and looked out of the window. How could anyone ever think he had eyes for another woman? Now that Irene didn't want him, he would never look at anyone else. Never.

'Jesus, Mary and Joseph!'

Boase and Rabone both looked up as the sound of breaking crockery reached their ears.

'Cook having a tantrum probably.' Rabone was grinning.

The aforementioned cook, a rotund woman of about forty, came running from the kitchen.

'Oh, gentlemen, please, can you help? It's Hilda – she's collapsed. Please come quickly.

Boase and Rabone ran into the kitchen where Hilda was just sitting herself up. Boase lifted her to her feet.

'Are you all right, Miss?'

Hilda Fox rubbed the back of her head and, looking at her hand, gasped when she saw a patch of red blood.

'Oh! I'm bleeding'

Boase looked at the back of her head.

'Don't worry miss – it's not too bad. Look, you must have banged your head on the corner of this cabinet when you fell. It'll be okay – here, take my handkerchief.'

Boase held his white handkerchief to the wound on Hilda's head.

'Oh – thank you. I don't know what happened. One minute I was buttering some bread the next…on the floor. Thank you so much. I'm all right now. Thank you.'

Mrs Tremayne, the cook, fetched Hilda's coat.

'Ere you are my girl. You get off 'ome. You're in no fit way to be 'ere. I can't 'ave girls collapsing in my kitchen – go on. Mind you're on time tomorrow. Run along now. You young women are always the same – won't eat nothing in case you get fat. Well, then before you know it, you're fainting. Fat didn't do me no 'arm – my 'usband says 'e likes a bit of something to grab 'old of. Sorry, gents – if you'd like to return to your table, Cissy will bring your food along.'

Boase and Rabone couldn't wait to escape that particular topic of conversation and were happy to oblige. Presently

Cissy, the object of Rabone's earlier interest, appeared with two plates of sandwiches.

The two men ate the food and stared out across the harbour in silence. Rabone spoke first. 'So – what do you reckon on the old lady's fish?'

'Oh…what? Sorry.'

Boase was watching the light fade and thinking about Irene.

'Sorry, Rabone. What with that distraction I forgot why we were here. I dunno – can't imagine anyone poisoning the food in here, can you? It's all in her mind. The old man probably ate something off that she cooked I expect. She got her free meals from it so I wouldn't bother any further. But we can tell her we've been in – that's not a lie, is it?'

Rabone nodded.

'Righty 'o. Whatever you say.'

Chapter Two

'But Doctor – Phillip is always in good health. I don't understand it. He's never sick. I don't understand about these stomach aches – four days now it's been.'

Dora Andrew swept her son's fringe from his eyes and drew him closer to her on her lap.

'Mrs Andrew – children pick up all sorts of things from their school and from their friends. It's part of growing up.'

Dr Richards sat back in his chair.

'Well, I have examined Phillip and I see nothing to indicate that he has anything other than a bit of a stomach upset. I suggest you keep an eye on him, let him stay off school for a couple of days – if he's still unwell on Tuesday come back and see me again.'

'Well, I'm not very happy Doctor, not happy.'

'Well, that's up to you – you are his mother but I am his doctor. I am giving you advice based on twenty five years in my profession. Good day, Mrs Andrew. Bye, Phillip.'

'Come in Boase – have a seat.'

Archie Boase sat down in Superintendent James Bolton's office.

'Look, I'm sorry the way things have turned out but I want you to know that George Bartlett is already being missed in this station and…'

'I know that, Sir. I'm missing him around very much.'

'I realise that. I just wanted to say that his replacement has been delayed and so I'm afraid that I will be depending on you and your skills for a while longer. You've done a fine job, Boase, since George left, and I'm sorry it's fallen to you. I can understand you must feel under pressure but your efforts will not have gone unnoticed. You've done well.'

'Thank you, Sir. I've been doing my best.'

'I know – and if you could just continue a while longer in your present capacity, I'm sure George's replacement will be very suitable indeed.'

'Yes, Sir. Thank you, Sir.'

Boase left Bolton's office feeling dismayed. He didn't like his present level of responsibility and, more, he didn't like George Bartlett not being around. Yes, he'd had invitations to his house, but how could he go there – what if he saw Irene? Yet, what if he didn't see Irene? Anyway, that aside, he wanted George Bartlett here, in this very station, working together like they always had. But that was never going to happen. As Boase pulled open the bottom drawer in his desk looking for something to graze on, Constable Penhaligon knocked on the door.

'I'm sorry to interrupt you, Archie, but we've had a complaint about some food that was consumed in George's Café – a woman left a message this morning. Mrs Laity she said her name was…must be that woman that came in here before to tell you her husband had been poisoned…'

'Oh, Lord, not her again! Yes, she was in here with a piece of rancid fish which I can still actually smell in the lobby. What now, Penhaligon?'

'Well, apparently, Percy Laity is up the hospital suffering badly from food poisoning – possibly not expected to recover.'

'You jest!'

Boase jumped up and grabbed his coat from the peg. Within ten minutes he was at the hospital at the top of Killigrew Street.

He approached a nurse who was walking towards him with a bundle of sheets in her arms.

'Excuse me, Nurse – could I please see the doctor who is treating Mr Laity?'

'Yes – of course. Sit here please and I'll see if Dr Masters can see you.'

'Thank you, Nurse.'

Boase sat and waited, looking across the corridor and out of the French doors which gave onto the gardens. After a few minutes Dr Masters appeared. Boase stood.

'Good morning, Doctor. I'm Constable Boase – I've been asked to speak to you about Percy Laity. I have information that he may be suffering from food poisoning?'

'Good morning, Constable – yes, he was indeed. Here's my office, do come in.'

Dr Masters led Boase into a small room off the corridor. It was minimally furnished with a desk, two chairs and a chest of drawers. Pictures of various anatomies hung from the white walls and in one corner stood a skeleton.

'What can you tell me about Mr Laity, Doctor?'

'Well, with no wish to be brutal, Constable, I can tell you that Mr Percy Laity died twenty minutes ago.'

'Died? *Died?* How did he die?'

Boase stood and leaned over the Doctor's desk.

'Well, as you already know – he was poisoned.'

'Yes…but…*died?*'

'I'm afraid so – I'm very sorry. Presumably you will now investigate this matter?'

'Well, yes – of course. What about Mrs Laity?'

'She was with him when he died – she's just left to be with her son.'

'Right. She left a message first thing this morning at the station. That's why I'm here.'

'Yes, I know. She asked to telephone from here.'

'Thank you for your time, Doctor Masters – I may need to see you again. Have you any idea of what poisoned him – what substance?'

'No, not yet – it's too early to say. The symptoms were indicative of several toxic substances. I can't tell you any more at the moment, Constable. I'm sorry.'

'Thank you.'

Boase left and took the walk back to the police station.

Superintendent Bolton met Boase as he walked into the station.

'Ah, Boase. I've just heard from the hospital about the Laity chap. How did you go on?'

'Well Sir, the doctor just said he couldn't tell me anything until they'd done more investigations, but that the man definitely died due to poisoning.'

'And this is the husband of the woman who came in complaining of the same recently, is it not?'

'Yes, Sir. Yes it is. I'm sorry, Sir – we went to George's Café to have a look round the same day but, well, there was nothing unremarkable or suspicious that we could see.'

'Don't worry, Boase – but we need to investigate this further. Of course, there may be nothing to be found at George's so, obviously we need to find out just what Mr Laity has been up to. I'll be needing you to lead this Boase…'

'…but, Sir…'

'Boase – you have a good brain for police work and, better still, you've had a very good teacher in George Bartlett. I have no other man for the job – and I will see that you are rewarded appropriately. I'll put together a team for you and I want you on this case now.'

'Very good, Sir.'

Boase sat at his desk not quite knowing where to begin. He didn't want this responsibility. No, not a bit if it. He just wanted things back how they used to be after the war. He ate a piece of fruit cake which he had earlier pulled from his pocket and thought. Where to start? What would George Bartlett do in this situation? Boase wandered over to the window, looked onto the street below and finished his cake, having decided that Bartlett would probably go straight to Mrs Laity. Yes. That might be a good start.

Irene Bartlett looked in the hall mirror, patted her hair straight and smoothed the front of her skirt. At that moment, there came a knock at the front door. Topper, the Airedale Terrier, sprang from his bed under the stairs and ran to the door, barking loudly. Irene grabbed her hat from the hall stand and opened the front door.

'Michael. How prompt you are. Are you looking forward to the recital?'

Michael Trelease touched the brim of his hat and awkwardly thrust a bunch of carnations into Irene's hand. The latest beau to call on Irene Bartlett was a good three inches shorter than the object of his desire, portly and with mousey, greased-back hair. Topper, who had been vigorously wagging his tail, now ceased wagging and barking and began to curl his lip. He let out a low growl.

'Topper, you remember Michael, don't be so unfriendly now. I'm sorry, Michael, he isn't usually like this. Try patting his head.'

As Michael Trelease gingerly put his hand forward and in Topper's direction, the dog met him half way with bared teeth, a snarl and a sharp nip on the thumb. Michael recoiled.

'Oh! I say, Irene – why did you make me do that? You know I don't like dogs – now look what the blighter has done. He's drawn blood.'

Irene took a floral handkerchief from her pocket and dabbed the tiny cut on Michael's thumb.

'You shouldn't be so nervous around Topper. He'll be fine when he gets to know you better. Come now – it's nothing. Shall we go then?'

Irene called out to the parlour.

'I won't be late Mum – but no need to wait up, I have my key.'

The front door clicked shut and the couple made their way out through the garden and onto Penmere Hill. Michael unwound the floral handkerchief and examined his wound.

'Blasted creature. You really need to take that dog in hand, Irene. He's a menace.'

'Oh, do shut up, Michael. It was nothing.'

The pair continued in silence to the large house on Melvill Road where the recital was to be held. The last time Irene had walked along this road was with Archie Boase, her fiancé. As they drew nearer to Boase's lodgings, Irene buried her face in Michael's shoulder and, after they had left the house behind, she turned and gave a quick backward glance.

George Bartlett topped up his glass with Leonard's London beer. He tapped his pipe on the fireplace and lifted his feet onto a small footstool.

'Topper does not like that young man Irene is hanging around with, Princess.'

Caroline Bartlett looked up from her mending.

'George, she is not hanging around with him – they're courting.'

'Well, I don't like him – he's got nothing about him, nothing to recommend him. Anyhow, she's on the rebound. What do you mean, courting? It's only a few months since she was with Boase – she didn't let the grass grow.'

'George! Take that back this instant. What a horrible thing to say about your daughter.'

'Well, I can't take this one seriously – and it's making her look desperate. She's barely known him five minutes and there they are, arm in arm. He never says a word to me you know. Won't come in the house, won't sit and have a drop of beer with me. Won't even come to tea.'

'Yes, I know, dear. I've invited him more than once. But, he's Irene's choice.'

'Well, there's a lot to be said for these arranged marriages you hear about abroad – sometimes the parents know best.'

Caroline Bartlett rose from her chair, threw her mending down and stood before her husband.

'George Bartlett. I have had quite enough of this now. Who said anything about marriage? Why are you carrying on and on? My word! You've changed since you've been out of work and...'

'I am not out of work as you put it and I'll thank you to remember that. You know perfectly well the reasons I am here with you now instead of where I should be, in my rightful place. So stop moaning!'

At that, Caroline burst into tears. It was the first time Bartlett had raised his voice in front of her in many years.

'Well you are turning into a horrible man – I'm not surprised they got rid of you – oh! Now look what you've made me say. George, I'm so sorry...'

Bartlett took his wife's small, slender hand and wrapping his large fingers around it, kissed her wedding ring.

'No, Princess, I should be sorry – it's not your fault all this has happened. I'd be lying if I said I didn't miss the place. Feel like I don't belong anywhere, have no purpose. The police force has been a large part of my life for so many years.'

'I know, dear – and I think I understand. But, George, you have to accept it, and, really, in the long run it might be better for you. You've worked so hard for so many years, maybe it's time for you to slow down a bit now.'

'I can't. It's not in my nature – you know that.'

'Yes, dear, I do – but you just have to accept it.'

George Bartlett sipped his beer and Caroline returned to her mending.

Michael and Irene strolled through the main streets of Falmouth, arm in arm.

'I hope you don't mind the long walk, Irene – but I don't want to let you go home. Did you enjoy the recital, dear?'

'Yes, very much thank you, Michael – did you?'

'I confess I did – more than I expected. Mind you I could have done without that awful Tregilgas woman coughing away behind us. It was incessant.'

'Yes, she did rather ruin it. But it was lovely all the same.'

'Would you like to go into the Rose Tearooms for supper, Irene?'

'Oh, Michael – we only went there yesterday and it's hugely expensive.'

'But you love it and we're almost there now.'

'Yes, I do. Thank you that would be lovely.'

Michael and Irene entered the Rose Tearooms and Restaurant in High Street and a chatty waitress led them to a window seat which looked out across Falmouth Harbour.'

'What would you like, Irene?'

'Umm...well, I really enjoyed that chicken thing we had yesterday...what was it called?'

'My dear – if you had it yesterday, tonight choose something different. Be adventurous.'

Irene scanned the menu until she found what she was looking for. Unable to pronounce it, she held the menu up to the waitress and pointed.

'May I have this, please?'

Her companion scowled.

'Waitress, what do you recommend?'

The waitress seeing Irene's discomfort took the menu from her.

'Chef recommends the chicken dish that you had last night, Miss. I don't mind it myself.'

Michael sighed very audibly.

'Well then, I think I'll have the same, waitress, please. And a bottle of wine.'

'Michael – you know I don't drink.'

'Yes you do my dear, a little. I know you do. Anyhow – a little of what you fancy does you good.'

Irene giggled and sat back in her seat.

The meal finished, Michael fetched Irene's coat from the stand in the lobby and held it up for her to slip on. As she turned, she observed a small mahogany cabinet on the wall. She went over and peered through the glass. Michael stood behind her.

'Seen something you like, my dear?'

'Oh, not really – I was just looking.'

'…at that rather enormous box of Turkish Delight I'd say. Miss – could we have this box of Turkish Delight please, yes, the large one.'

The waitress opened the cabinet and handed the box to Michael.'

'No – this is for my lady, thank you. Here you are, Irene.'

Irene took the box and kissed Michael on the cheek.

'Michael, thank you – but this is so expensive.'

'It's only money, my dear, only money.'

The couple left the Rose Tearooms, Irene tightly clutching the precious box and feeling selfish for choosing it, in the knowledge that her parents couldn't abide Turkish Delight.

Archie Boase took Constable Eddy to Mrs Laity's house on Budock Terrace. Mrs Laity was just unlocking the door whilst struggling with a heavy bag of shopping. Boase rushed forward.

'Can I help you Mrs Laity?'

The woman turned, startled.

'No – thank you. I can manage.

'Mrs Laity – I'm Constable Boase. Do you remember me? You brought me the fish, into the police station.

'Oh – you. Yes, of course I remember. What do you want?'

'I'm so sorry for the loss of your husband, Mrs Laity. I was wondering if I could talk to you please?'

'What is there to talk about? Percy's dead.'

'Please may we come in – just for a few moments?'

'Come on then. In you come.'

Mrs Laity held open the door for the two men and all three went through to the parlour.

'Before you say anything, I know Percy was poisoned.'

'Yes, Mrs Laity. But, of course, we need to investigate what happened.'

'I know – why do you think I came to see you? Yet you did nothing.'

'But why do you think anyone would want to poison your husband? He was a likeable and well known man as far as I can see.'

'Yes. Yes 'e was. But somebody didn't like 'im – did they, Constable?'

'I can assure you, Mrs Laity, that we will do everything we can to find out what happened. I need you to explain exactly what happened both times you went out to eat. Please tell me everything you can – what you had, did you notice what anyone else was eating – has anyone you know also complained of feeling unwell?'

'Oh, so many questions, young man.'

'Please tell me as much as you can, Mrs Laity. It's very important.'

The woman sat at her kitchen table and recalled as many of the events as she could. Boase wrote quickly in his notebook as she spoke.

'You've been very helpful, Mrs Laity. Thank you. I may need to come back and see you again if that's all right?'

'As you wish.'

'I'm so sorry about everything, Mrs Laity, very sorry.'

Boase and Eddy left the small terraced house and walked back to the police station. They chatted as they walked.

'I don't know how to deal with this, Eddy – I don't have the experience. I don't have the right credentials.'

'But Superintendent Bolton believes in you and he wants you to do this. What would Inspector Bartlett do?'

'That's what I keep asking myself – but I don't know the answer.'

'But you do – you worked with him long enough. You can do it.'

'Thanks – I wish I had the same amount of confidence in me as you seem to have.'

At the Bartlett house, Topper sat with his favourite rubber ball in his mouth and looked up at his master, his head cocked enquiringly to one side. George Bartlett regarded him as he walked through to the parlour.

'You wouldn't be asking for a walk by any chance would you, my boy? But it's raining...look.'

Bartlett held open the front door and Topper and he looked out onto the front garden and the road beyond. It had been raining heavily for several hours.

'There you are – you didn't believe me, did you?'

Caroline came out into the hall.

'What are you two chatting about?'

'Oh, just the weather, Princess. He wants to go out in it.'

'Well – you do have a new raincoat which needs testing, dear.'

'Trying to get rid of me?'

Bartlett nodded his head towards the cup and saucer Caroline was holding.

'That cuppa for me?'

'Certainly not – Irene is having a little rest. She's saying she feels a bit unwell so I'm taking her some tea.'

'Unwell? I'm not surprised – probably all that confectionery she shovelled in last night...and burning the candle at both ends. No good will come of it I tell you.'

'Oh, do stop, George dear. She didn't eat much – it's probably just the strain, what with one thing and another.'

'Hmmm – well, you know my opinion; the sooner she gets rid of that piece of dead wood, the better.'

'George! Don't be like that – she and Michael get along just fine. Don't ruin it for them. Now come on, the tea is getting cold while I'm passing the time of day here with you.'

'Well, I don't like him. And another thing, where does he get all his money from? I never see him doing anything, a job of work - tell me that...'

'Shhhh – George, she'll hear you. Stop it.'

Caroline went upstairs and George looked at Topper who had now dropped the ball at his master's feet. Bartlett stooped and picked it up.

'Right, if we go, then you carry it – and don't lose it.'

Topper's joy knew no bounds and he leapt up and down in the hallway.

'Careful, you always do this to your mother's rug – she'll tell me off, not you.'

Bartlett straightened the dishevelled rug, put on his new raincoat and hat and clipped Topper's lead to his collar.

'Off we go then, come on – not long mind.'

Chapter Three

'Come in, Boase, have a seat.'

Superintendent Bolton was standing at the window in his office. He coughed and sat on the corner of his desk.

'I'm sorry if you're feeling a little neglected, Archie – we're so stretched at the moment and I know you're feeling it more than most but I really appreciate what you're doing for us.'

'Happy to help, Sir.'

'What's the latest? Any updates?'

'Yes. Actually, Sir, I was just about to go up to the hospital – we've had word that they have news on Percy Laity's poisoning. I suppose if we can find the substance then it might help to narrow down our search.'

'Precisely. However, tread carefully – depending on the result, this could be an innocent mistake – or something more sinister. Keep me posted and I'll help if I can.'

'Thank you, Sir. I will. Oh – just one other thing, Sir, there's been another admission to the hospital due to poisoning. Last night as a matter of fact.'

'Well that puts a different complexion on things then. You'd better cut along as soon as you can – don't let me hold you up any further.'

'Yes, Sir – thank you, Sir.'

Edgar Villiers held a cup up to his wife's mouth.

'Come along, darling - be a good girl now. Drink some tea. There, that's the ticket.'

Eunice Villiers stared, wide-eyed into the distance as the tea trickled down from the corners of her mouth.

'Blast you, Eunice – just drink the tea! I don't have much time.'

A tear formed in the woman's eye and she turned and looked at her husband. He took her small, pale hand in his.

'Darling – forgive me, I'm sorry. I just wanted you to have something to drink. Do you remember, my dear, when we had Agnes doing for us? And you shouted at her every day because she couldn't make a cup of tea to save her life? Do you remember, dearest girl?'

Eunice showed no flicker of emotion, or even recognition, as her pale blue eyes stared into her husband's.

'Come along now, Sir. Mr Villiers – it's time to go. I'll take care of your wife now. Come along. We'll see you on Thursday as usual, shall we?'

'Yes, Matron. Of course, Thursday as usual. Good day.'

Edgar walked across the drive to his car and turned, looking back and up at his wife's window on the first floor of the Meadowbank Home for the Insane. Set on a quiet lane on the outskirts of Redruth, the Victorian house was imposing and dour. It had been a lunatic asylum in its earlier days but now was more of a medical facility to care for those deemed to be not in their right mind. Edgar thought how beautiful the name Meadowbank sounded and how, in reality, it was such an ugly place. But still, he blamed himself, in part for his wife's fate. And yet, no. She was entirely to blame for being locked up in here. Yes, it was all her fault. His thoughts were interrupted by the shrill voice of a woman.

'Do hurry Edgar, darling. We're going to be so late for the Prendergast's dinner.'

Edgar, reaching his car, slid into the driver's seat next to Topsy Beaufort.

'How is the old cow?'

'Topsy, I've asked you before…don't speak about Eunice like that.'

'Why? You don't even like her. In fact, I don't know why you've had the nerve to bring me here. I could have gone sailing with Plumpy Dawson and his sister.'

'No you couldn't – the weather is inclement and in any case, you agreed to come so that we could go on to the Prendergast's from here as it's on our way. Now please, just stop.'

Topsy, realising she had said too much, pulled a compact from her bag and began applying a bright red lipstick to her mouth. She looked at Edgar.

'Is this too red, darling?'

She pouted.

'I don't know, I'm trying to keep my eyes on the road.'

'You never look at me.'

Topsy sat back in her seat and decided to say nothing for the rest of the journey.

Archie Boase sat in the lobby at the hospital, waiting to see Dr Masters about his findings on Percy Laity and the poison. He waited for over half an hour. A nurse came past and he stopped her.

'Excuse me, Nurse. I'm waiting to see Dr Masters – is he available yet?'

'I'm sorry, Dr Masters had to go out to see a patient – he's not going to be back in the hospital today. Did you have an appointment to see him?'

'No, not exactly – but I did say I'd be here about now. It's about Percy Laity. Is there anyone else I can talk to about him?'

'No, I'm sorry – he did say he was expecting someone from the police here – that'll be you then?'

'Oh – yes, I'm so sorry. Forgive me. I'm Constable Archie Boase.'

Boase offered his hand to the nurse and she smiled and placed hers inside.

'There isn't anyone else you can speak to Constable…Dr Masters is dealing with this himself.'

'That's okay – don't worry. I'll come back in the morning; will he be here then?'

'Of course. See you tomorrow then?'

'Yes – oh, and please call me Archie.'

The nurse blushed.

'I'm Phyllis – but everyone calls me Phyll.'

'Thank you – um, Phyll. Goodbye.'

Boase left the hospital, his heart racing but he didn't know why. What an idiot! He was imagining how stupid he must have sounded *'please call me Archie.'* What a clot he was.

Feeling hungry and knowing there was no debris to graze on in his desk drawer, unusually Boase decided to drop into the Seven Stars for a drink and a sandwich. He was entitled to a half an hour break but rarely took one. He passed the police station and went on to the public house where he had often sat discussing work with George Bartlett. In fact, this was the first time he had been in here without him. He went to the bar, not recognising anyone working in there. He ordered a small beer and a cheese sandwich and took them to a table in the corner of the room. Yes, indeed it was strange being here without Bartlett. Boase ate his lunch thinking about the older man – how he always moaned about the beer, *every single time* and then about the prices – you could depend on it. Boase was feeling lonely and out of his depth. He thought about the nurse he'd just embarrassed himself in front of. She was rather pretty, but she didn't smell of lilacs as far as he could tell – and when she had smiled, her nose didn't wrinkle…he'd looked for it. Boase finished his sandwich and small beer and went back to work. He couldn't progress with his enquiry until he had spoken to the doctor – and he had lots of work piled on his desk to deal with. He'd start again first thing tomorrow.

'Mummy…Mummy! My stomach's bursting…'
'Oh! My Lord – it's okay, Phillip – Mummy's here.'
Dora Andrew held a bucket next to her son's bed as he vomited profusely.
'Bert…BERT! Quickly fetch a doctor…run like the wind!'
Bert Andrew grabbed his jacket from the hall stand and ran from the house. The nearest doctor he knew of was Dr Glendenning on Western Terrace, about a three or four minute run from their home at Clifton Place. Dr Glendenning came immediately and brought Bert Andrew with him in his car. As they entered the house, Phillip was screaming and crying. The two men ran up the stairs to find the boy in his mother's arms.
'Oh Doctor – thank you so much for coming so quickly…he's been so ill. Dr Masters said it was normal…'
'No, Mrs Andrew – this is most definitely not normal – this child is going to be admitted to hospital immediately.'

Within thirty minutes Phillip Andrew was lying in a hospital bed.

The heavy rain Falmouth had experienced earlier returned overnight. Boase couldn't sleep. Irene was on his mind. He felt like a cheat – he had talked to Phyll…and he had enjoyed the brief interlude which, if he was honest, had momentarily brightened up his day. He sat up in his single bed and pushed back the eiderdown. The little clock showed it was only twenty minutes to midnight. He took a sip of water from the glass on the nightstand and propped himself up on his pillows. How could he feel like a cheat? There was nothing between himself and Irene any longer – he had seen to that with his foolishness and his arrogant pride. He hadn't seen her for months. He wondered if she still wore the bracelet he had given her on their first Christmas. He wondered if her hair had grown; that was what started the rot – all over her hair. But he could see now that she was right – if she wanted to cut off her beautiful long hair then it was her choice. If she wanted to shave her head, what business was it of his? He slumped back on his pillows, stared at the ceiling and watched the rain drizzling down the window between the half open curtains.

At half past one, Boase pulled on his trousers, shoes and a sweater and, grabbing his raincoat from the hall stand, left quietly by the side door. He walked up Melvill Road, along Western Terrace and in the direction of Penmere Hill. Arriving at the Bartlett's house, he sat on the wall in the rain and looked up at Irene's bedroom window. The room was in darkness. He wondered if she was awake. He wondered if she was thinking of him like he was of her. The rain was falling heavier now and Boase pulled his collar higher. He missed her. But she probably had someone else now – someone better looking, someone with money - but not someone who had loved her like he had – like he still loved her, no, that would never happen. But he'd ruined everything with his foolishness – there was no going back now.

Boase walked to Castle Beach and stood looking out across the bay thinking how his life had changed so much over the last few months. He had lost his boss who was also a friend and mentor and he'd lost the love of his life. Now he was doing a job he didn't feel capable of and worried he'd mess that up too. What else could go wrong!

Boase returned home and finally got into bed at half past four – but still sleep didn't come and by a quarter to eight he was at his desk. He quickly drank a cup of cold tea, checked his diary for the day and headed back up to the hospital to speak to Dr Masters about the poisoning of Percy Laity.

'Dr Masters will see you now.'

A nurse opened the door to a small consulting room where Dr Masters sat behind an oak desk piled high with papers. He rose from his seat and offered Boase his hand.

'Good morning, so sorry I wasn't here to see you yesterday.'

'Oh, that's quite all right, Doctor. I just wanted to ask about your findings in respect of Mr Laity – oh, and I hear you have another possible casualty?'

'Yes, quite. Please – do sit.'

Boase pulled a chair up to the desk and sat opposite the doctor.

'Cigarette?'

'Oh – no thank you, Sir. I don't really smoke.'

'Probably just as well – they say it's good for one's lungs but, well, I don't see how that can be the case. Still, never mind. Now – Mr Laity. Well, we've had some results back and, indeed, he was poisoned. Thallium.'

Boase leaned forward in his seat.

'Thallium?'

'Yes – I know. I was surprised too. But it fits with the symptoms the poor man had.'

'So – do you think it's suspicious, Sir?'

'Well, I'm afraid that's your territory. But, I can say, you would find it in present day rat poison, you know, pest control, that sort of thing – so you need to discover whether that was something Laity used maybe. But I understand from his wife that they ate a couple of times in local establishments – that may be a different kettle of fish, so to speak.'

'And did you say you had another case admitted?'

'Yes – a young boy, similar symptoms – admitted him last night, but he's showing a slight improvement. I've been treating him for the same – thallium toxicity and that seems be helping. I say treating, nothing more than making sure he excretes as much of everything from his body as possible – he's improving but very weak now…my impression is that he has had a severe sickness episode and unrelated to the poison but I have treated him the same, as a worst case. I'll take you to see him if you like. And there's one other – not sure about her at the moment; not really treating so much as observing – the symptoms are slightly different but I'm keeping a close eye on her.'

Dr Masters took Boase to see Phillip Andrew who was sleeping soundly with his mother at his bedside. She stood up as Dr Masters introduced her to Boase.

'Mrs Andrew, I will be calling on you later to talk about what Phillip has been doing if that will be all right? Just to try to find out what's happened.'

'Yes, of course, Constable Boase. I'll be at home later on today – I just didn't like to leave him but the doctor says he's improving a little – thank God.'

'Indeed.'

Boase said goodbye to Dr Masters and to Mrs Andrew and left the hospital.

Within ten minutes, Boase was knocking at Mrs Laity's front door. The woman opened it and invited him into the parlour.

'Mrs Laity, I've discovered that your husband had ingested a poisonous substance…'

'I already told you that!'

'But we didn't know what it was, we now know it was thallium – and it was unlikely that the source of the poison was George's Café.'

'Well you don't know that.'

'Mrs Laity, I'm so sorry but before I do anything else I need to ask about your husband's habits.'

'What? What do you mean, 'is 'abits?'

'Well for example, you have a lovely garden – did he use poison during his gardening, or what about rats – did you have a vermin problem here?'

'Well, a couple of years ago we 'ad a biggun – came into the scullery, bold as you like. Percy saw 'im off, yes – 'e poisoned the blighter.'

'So, where would he have kept any poisonous substances?'

'In the shed – I'll show you.'

'Thank you, Mrs Laity.'

Boase followed the woman out to the garden and to a stone outbuilding – the 'shed.' It was very tidy; there were pots of paint, brushes, some oily rags and several tools. In one corner there was a shelf with a few small tins and bottles on it. Boase searched through them. There was no rat poison, no weed killer, nothing that could cause anyone any harm in here.'

'Mrs Laity, may I have a look under your kitchen sink, please?'

'Well, yes, but there's not much under there.'

Boase returned to the scullery and looked in the small cupboard. The woman was right – nothing here. He looked up at her from his kneeling position.

'Do you think anyone would want to hurt your husband?'

'No – no, absolutely not!'

'Right, thanks, Mrs Laity. We'll speak again soon.'

'Rabone, come with me back to the hospital, will you?'

Boase was slipping his coat on and finishing a rather bruised apple as he walked along the road. As the two men entered the front door of the hospital, Phyll appeared carrying a bunch of flowers. She smiled at Boase.

'Hello again.'

Boase felt his face burning as he looked at the nurse.

'Hello, Phyll – how nice to see you again.'

He turned as she walked past and into a nearby ward.

'You've gone red, Archie.'

'Shut up, Rabone.'

No one being about, Boase wandered along the corridor, peering through several doors hoping to catch Dr Masters again. He saw Phillip Andrew, propped up in bed and speaking to his mother. That was a relief all round he thought. As he rounded a corner and found himself in a smaller corridor, he saw Dr Masters talking to another doctor. Both men had their backs to him and they were chatting in low voices as they wandered away from him. Nevertheless, Boase had heard what they were saying.

'Yes, yes – I think it's thallium too – again. But this is severe, and if I'm honest, Rob, I'm not hopeful. Yes, I know – the Professor will be here this afternoon, yes, he's quite the expert. But it's worrying that she isn't seeing very well. She barely responded to our tests.'

The two doctors went into a room at the end of the corridor and closed the door behind them. Boase had now reached the ward where they had left the patient. The door was ajar. He peered inside. There was a nurse sitting on a chair with her back to him. He looked across at the bed. He recognised the cropped hair on the pillow. *Irene!*

Chapter Four

Boase continued to stare at the bed not sure what to do. Suddenly he flung the door wide open and burst into the room throwing himself across Irene's bed. He lifted her into her arms but she didn't move.

'Excuse me – what do you think you are doing? You can't come in here'!

The nurse pulled Boase's sleeve in an attempt to stop him.

'Doctor…DOCTOR, quickly!'

Dr Masters and the other he had been speaking with came running down the corridor and into the room in time to see Boase laying Irene back onto the bed. He turned to them, tears were in his eyes.

'Constable Boase, what on earth do you mean by this?'

Dr Masters pushed Boase out into the corridor and led him to his consulting room. He motioned to the other doctor to leave them. Boase sat on a chair, he head buried in his hands.

'What's happened to her? Is she going to be okay?'

'I can't really discuss that with you just now, Constable – as yet, this doesn't form part of your investigations and you're also not her next of kin.'

'I'm going to be…'

'Well, judging by your unprofessional reaction just then, I can see that you must know the girl – which is more than we do. She was found collapsed in the street this morning and we have no idea who she is. Can you help?'

Boase looked up at the doctor and rubbed the tears from his eyes.

'Her name is Irene Bartlett. She's my fiancée.'

'Oh – I'm so sorry. We had no idea. Does she have family?'

'Yes, she does. I'll go to them now and tell them she's here. They'll be worrying. What's wrong with her?'

'We think she, too, has been poisoned.'

'Oh, no! Please, no. How bad is it?'

'I can't really discuss that with you now – we're waiting for the Professor to arrive. He's more expert in this field. But you might like to bring her close family here. As soon as you can.'

'So…it's bad?'

'Like I said, I can't tell you any more just yet.'

Boase left the hospital, he felt like someone was rattling his brain around inside his head. He hadn't felt like this since…since, the war. He looked down at his shaking hands. Irene could die. She hadn't even known he was in the room. He crossed the road and walked towards Penmere Hill. He tried to think; all he could think was bad. What if his Irene died? How could he live without her? Why had he been so horrible and made her cry when he would do anything to make her happy? Boase didn't hear the motor car approach him as he crossed the street again. The car knocked him into the side of the road and a young man leaned out of the window and waved his fist. Boase lay half on and half off the pavement. He looked down and saw that his trousers were ripped around his left knee. He pulled himself upright aware that he was still shaking. He staggered on and towards the Bartlett's house. Almost falling through the gate he walked up to the front door and knocked repeatedly. He could hear Topper on the other side, barking madly. The door opened and there stood George Bartlett. He looked at the visitor.

'Boase...Boase, what's happened? Are you going to come in?'

Boase staggered through the hall and Bartlett closed the front door and followed him.

'Go on, go into the parlour.'

Bartlett looked at the other man and saw him shaking, saw the ripped trousers.

'Boase, have you been drinking?'

Archie Boase slumped down into an armchair, unable to speak for a moment. Bartlett knelt down beside him.

'What is it, what's happened – come on man, you're frightening the life out of me!'

Boase sat upright in the chair and looked into Bartlett's eyes.

'It's Irene – Sir, she's in hospital.'

'What are you talking about – why would she be in hospital?'

At that point, Caroline came into the parlour. She looked at the two men.

'George, Archie – what's going on? What's happened?'

'Sit down, Princess. It's Irene...'

'...oh no! What's happened? Where is she?'

'I'm sorry, Mrs Bartlett. Irene is up at the hospital. She's been poisoned.'

'Poisoned? Poisoned you say?' Caroline took her husband's hand in hers.

'George, take me to the hospital – we must go now.'

Caroline grabbed her coat from the hallstand and ran out into the garden and to the gate.

'Princess, don't you want your hat?'

'Come on George. Archie, hurry please.'

As the three rushed to the top of the hill, Caroline began to walk a little slower.

'Don't rush, Mrs Bartlett – here, give me your arm.'

Caroline and Boase walked together, he supporting her and they were soon entering the hospital.

Caroline ran to the nurse's station and spoke to a young doctor who was writing at the desk.

'I want to see my daughter – Miss Irene Bartlett. Where is she?'

'Just a minute please, Madam. I'll fetch the doctor who is looking after her.'

The young man walked down the corridor and returned within minutes with Doctor Masters. Bartlett stood behind his wife and Boase behind him.

'Mr and Mrs Bartlett? Would you like to step into consulting room?'

Boase watched as the group of three walked away from the desk. George Bartlett stopped, hesitated, and turned back.

'Come along, Boase – don't just stand there.'

Grateful to be included, Boase, who had thought he should leave Irene's parents alone with the doctor, followed after them and the four entered the room, Caroline and Doctor Masters seated and Bartlett and Boase standing. George Bartlett spoke first.

'We've just been told that our daughter has been poisoned…how? What happened? How bad is she?'

Doctor Masters leaned across his desk.

'Your daughter has ingested some toxic substance – have you any idea what it could have been?'

Bartlett now also leaned forward.

'Doctor, I don't wish to appear rude, but we want to know how bad our daughter is and, anyhow, how would we know what it could have been…'

'…George, dear, just wait. Doctor, we know that Irene had dinner out with a friend the night before last and she also brought home some chocolates. But, please…please may we see her?'

'Yes, of course, Mrs Bartlett – follow me.'

The group of four went into the room where Irene lay in bed. Caroline ran to her and clasped her hand.

'Irene, Irene, please wake up…it's Mum. Dad's here too.'

George Bartlett walked around to the other side of the bed and, bending over his daughter, kissed her forehead. Her mother looked up.

'Doctor, can't she even hear us?'

'Your daughter has been sedated, Mrs Bartlett, while we try to remove the poison from her body. Let us return to my room to talk further. As the three left the room, Boase moved from the door and over to the bed. He kissed Irene's hand and wiped his tears away from his cheek with her fingers.

'Irene, I bet you can hear me – although you never listen to anything I say, you little pixie. But you listen to this – and listen well. You are coming out of here and I'm going to take care of you. You're my girl and we're going to be married as soon as you're well again. For once you'll do as you're told…and I don't care about your hair; you do whatever you like with it but please, please my dearest, sweet girl – don't you ever leave me. I can't be without you. Don't you dare leave me. I have to go now but I'll be back soon to take you out of here as soon as you're ready…just don't leave it too long – you hear me?'

Boase kissed Irene's slender hand again and her soft, pale cheek. Turning back as he reached the door, he left. As he rounded the corner into the next corridor, the Bartlett's were saying goodbye to Doctor Masters. Boase saw the two men shake hands. Caroline was sobbing as they left the hospital and walked out into the garden. Boase ran to catch them up.

'What did the doctor say?'

Bartlett turned to him.

'It's bad news, Boase, very bad news.'

'What, Sir? What did he say? She is going to be okay, isn't she?'

'I don't know, my boy…we don't know. The doctor says he's waiting for another expert opinion but…but, at best and if she recovers from this…'

'…what, Sir? If she recovers, *what?*

'She'll be blind. She'll never be able to see again.'

At that, Caroline fell to the ground. The two men lifted her to her feet and sat her on a nearby bench.

'Come on, Princess, come on now – we have to be strong for our girl in there. Come on, stop this now.'

'George, she will never see us again, never. Archie…Archie…?'

Boase had already left. He couldn't listen to any more.

Marjorie Medlin sat up in bed. She looked at her husband sleeping.

'Ned. Ned…wake up, Ned I don't feel well.'

'What time is it, Marjorie?'

'It's almost half past six.'

'Go back to sleep for a bit.'

'Ned – I've got terrible pains in me stomach. I can't sleep. Please, Ned.'

'I'll go down and get you some water.'

Ned pulled on his trousers which had been on the back of the chair next to the bed and, braces hanging by his sides, he went downstairs to the scullery. The children were still asleep and he moved around quietly so as not to wake them. He filled a glass with water from the tap and took a box of aspirin from the little cupboard over the sink. Slowly he climbed the stairs and entered the bedroom.

'Here you are, Doll. Got some tablets for you.'

He pulled back the eiderdown to return to bed and gasped.

'Marjorie, Marjorie love, what's happened?'

His wife looked at the sheet she was laying on; it was drenched with blood.

'Oh my God. Ned, 'elp me.'

'All right, what shall I do? What's happened?'

'Oh, Ned, I don't know. Can you get someone to come? Can you get someone?'

'WHO? Who shall I get?'

'Your Mother – she'll know what to do. Please go quickly.'

Boase sat at Bartlett's desk and looked out of the window onto the street below. He thought about the last twelve months and how things had changed. How different things were when he and Irene were happy. All the plans they'd made, marriage, a little house, maybe children. For the first time, and in his new position, Boase was actually able to afford to take care of Irene properly now. Yes, he had enough money – but what if she could never see again? She would never see the little blue chair by the fireside he had promised her – or the wedding ring she kept looking at in the Church Street Jewellers window. She said she loved it because it looked like little waves had been cut into the band, she said it reminded her of the sea. Boase would buy that – he'd kept looking at it, it was still in the window. But Irene might never see it. And then, worse, what if she never woke up? A tear fell onto Boase's lapel. He jumped as a sharp knock on the door sounded like a clap of thunder and interrupted his thoughts. The door opened and Penhaligon stood there.

'Thought you might like a cuppa? You do know it's not even seven yet?'

'Oh – that's kind of you, thanks, Penhaligon. Yes, I know but I've got plenty to do.'

Ned Medlin banged on the door and the windows of the Well Lane surgery which was shared by Dr Haskins and Dr Mitchelmore. There was no reply. This was the nearest doctor. He ran his fingers through his hair and thought. He could try Dr Cook on Florence Terrace but that would take too long to get there. As he stood and thought what would be for the best, Ned's brother, Saul, came round the corner at top speed on his bicycle. Ned jumped out into his path almost knocking them both to the ground.

'Watch out, Ned – what on earth are you doing? I'm late for me shift'

'Quickly, it's Marjorie – she needs a doctor. There's no one in here…please can you bicycle over to Dr Cook's place? Ask him to come to her…please, Saul. Don't hang about, please.'

'I'm on me way…you go 'ome!'

Saul's voice disappeared into the distance as he cycled away. Ned ran back to the house. He entered the hall and looked at the clock. It was five to seven. He climbed the stairs and went into the bedroom. Marjorie lay on the bed, her back to him. He leaned over and touched her shoulder.

'Marjorie. Marj, love. Dr Cook is coming to help you. You awake?'

Ned pulled his wife towards him and stared into her face. Her eyes were wide open and he face as white as snow. He shook her.

'Marjorie. My God…MARJORIE!'

As he sat on the bed with his wife's head on his chest, he heard the front door open downstairs.

'Ned…Ned? You up there?'

Ned didn't answer his brother's call but sat, motionless. He heard two sets of footsteps on the wooden stairs and looked up as Saul and Dr Cook entered the room. The doctor walked around the bed and looked at the woman.

'It's all right, Mr Medlin – you can let go. Please now, I need to see your wife. Why don't you let your brother make you a cup of sweet tea? Go on now. Both of you.'

Saul led his brother, who had still not spoken, down to the scullery where he set about boiling a kettle of water to make some tea. The brothers sat for some time in silence. Presently Dr Cook's footsteps were heard descending the staircase and he came into the scullery. He joined the two men at the small table.

'Ned. I have some bad news for you.'

'I know, she's dead. I felt her.'

'Do you know what made your wife unwell?'

'No.'

'Well, I don't want to trouble you too much just now but, did you know…did you know Marjorie was expecting a baby?'

At that, Ned looked up, his eyes filled with tears.

'No, Doctor, no, Sir, I didn't. She never said. Oh, my Lord…another baby. Is the baby dead too?'

'Yes, Ned – she wasn't very far gone. I'm sorry.'

Dr Cook laid his hand on Saul's shoulder.

'Can you stay with him please? I will make the necessary arrangements.'

Saul nodded and showed Dr Cook to the door.

Archie Boase sat in Superintendent Bolton's office.

'Boase, I'm getting a bit worried about these poisonings…and I'm so sorry to hear about Irene, by the way. If there's anything I can do…'

'…no one can do anything, Sir. But thank you.'

'Well, I know this isn't going to be easy for you with everything that's going on in your personal life but I hope you'll be able to stick with it and sort this mess out. You're doing so well – I'm very proud to have you on the team.

'Thank you, Sir.'

'If you need anything, then just ask. If I can do it, I will. Now please get on as best you can and let's get to the bottom of this.'

Boase left and shut the door behind him. He didn't feel confident like all the others did. What would Bartlett do?

Topsy Beaufort swam to the side of Sebastian and Millicent Prendergast's pool. She rested her arms on the side.

'Edgar, darling – do pass me a towel. Hurry, I'm getting cold.'

Edgar Villiers obliged, holding the towel as Topsy climbed the steps and stood on the terrace.

'It's getting rather chilly, darling – is this the largest towel you could find?'

'Yes, my dear – it's all there was. Don't make a fuss now.'

Topsy scowled as she pulled the bathing cap from her head and ran her fingers through her auburn curls. The pair had spent two days with the Prendergasts at their country Estate on the Roseland Peninsula. The house was large and the vast grounds sprawled from the gardens down to a small private landing point with a jetty on the river and where the Prendergasts moored two or three boats.

'I'm going in to change for dinner. Remember the four of us are going out this evening, Edgar.'

'Are we? I had no idea. I was hoping for a quiet evening in.'

'Edgar – you are simply too boring.'

This was not the first time this topic of conversation had come up; Edgar Villiers was a married man of forty-six, Topsy a young, vibrant woman of twenty-five.

'You didn't tell me we were dining out. No one did. Where are we going?'

'We're meeting Plumpy Dawson and his cousin, Theo. He's just visiting from Scotland. They've arranged for us to take a boat over to Falmouth and we're dining on the Mermaid.'

'The Mermaid? Absolutely nothing doing, Topsy, my girl. We are not dining on the Mermaid. That is the last word on the subject.'

Edgar walked from the pool and back up to the house. Topsy had noticed how, when he was angry, the corner of his mouth twitched. She put on her shoes and followed him back to the house.

The Mermaid was a floating restaurant – a vessel that most evenings, and given the right conditions, sailed up the river from Falmouth to Truro and dropped anchor in a small creek along the way while guests dined on board. Topsy had never been on this trip and had so much been looking forward to it. She went to her room and began hunting for a dress; she would jolly well go on the Mermaid trip, with Edgar Villiers or without him! As she searched for some shoes, there was a light knock on the door and it half opened. Edgar stuck his head around the door.

'Topsy, darling…don't be such a silly thing. Come on now, my sweet – why don't we go elsewhere? Just you and me – please say yes.'

'I want to go on the Mermaid with my friends – why can't we? Is it because you're frightened that Dorothy Passmore will be there with her new husband? Is that why we can't go?'

'That's a ridiculous thing to say – and she is very much in the past, why, even before Eunice.'

'Well, I heard she jilted you and Eunice was second best – and you can't forget her.'

'Topsy, darling – you're overwrought. Stop this now. I don't want to go and so we will do something else.'

'You can't stop me and I'm going.'

Boase left work and began the walk back to his lodgings. The day had been a long one. Philip Andrew was returning to school on Monday...that wasn't poison, just very bad sickness. His landlady, Mrs Curgenven would have his supper ready. Friday. Fish pie on Fridays. Boase felt hungry but as though he couldn't eat anything. Mrs Curgenven's fish pie was one of Boase's favourite meals. Fish? Poor Percy Laity had fish. Boase kept thinking. If the fish had been poisoned, how? Who would do that? Why? Superintendent Bolton was rather irritated to find that the fish had not been examined but the day it was received into the police station, no one had dreamed what would happen next. The fish was stinking and had been thrown out.

On reaching the top of Killigrew, Boase sat on the hospital wall. He was still in pain from where the motor car had struck him – but he had not sought medical attention. He thought about Irene inside the hospital. He looked over his shoulder and towards her window. What could he do? He had to get her back. He had to find out who had hurt her. He had to find out who killed Percy Laity. So much to do and yet where to start? As he pulled a boiled sweet from his pocket and put it into his mouth, he heard a shout.
'Boase...Boase, wait there.'
He looked across the road and saw George Bartlett and Caroline walking towards him. Boase stood up as the couple approached him.
'You just knocked off, my boy?'
'Yes, sir. I'm just on my way home...been a long day.'
'Yes, I'm sure it has. We're just going in to see Irene.'
'Have you had any news, Sir? About anything they can do?'

'No, it's still not looking good – but, where there's life there's hope. That's the only thing we can keep telling ourselves. They let Caroline come up this morning and help to wash her and talk to her. I think they're hoping that might help a little.'

'Archie – she knew it was me…she put her hand up and touched my hair. She knew I was there.'

'That's good to know.'

Boase's voice cracked a little.

'Look, my boy, why don't you come and have a bit of supper with us later? Be nice to see you in the house again.'

'Well, my supper will be waiting when I get back.'

'All right then – come and have a drop of beer with me, keep me company.'

'That would be rather nice, thank you – getting a bit sick of my own company if I'm honest.'

'That's settled then – come at eight?'

'It would be lovely to see you at home, Archie.'

Caroline squeezed Boase's arm and the couple went across the gardens and into the hospital.

Topper jumped up and down in the hall as Boase knocked at the front door. Caroline held the dog's collar as she pulled the door open.

'Hello, Archie – I'm so glad you came. Come in. Topper – stop getting so excited.'

Boase went into the parlour where George Bartlett was smoking his pipe. Two bottles of Leonard's London Beer were on the side table with two glasses.

'Draw up a chair, Boase and you can tell me all about it.'

Boase obliged and Topper sat by his feet.

'What news of Irene, Sir?'

'No change, Boase. No change since earlier. But we must keep hope. Of course, we'll let you know if there is any news, won't we, Princess?'

'Yes, we will, Archie.'

At that, Boase broke down and sobbed.

'I'm so sorry – for everything that's happened. I feel like it's all my fault. I was so horrible to her. She didn't deserve that.'

'It's no one's fault, my boy, stop thinking that. Now, tell me all your news.'

'Well that's another thing. I'm really in a hole, I don't mind telling you. Superintendent Bolton has put me in charge and I really don't know which way to turn.'

'Want to talk about it?'

'I wish you could come back, Sir, I really do. It's just not the same without you.'

'Well, I don't think that's on the cards – but tell me all about it…let's see if I can offer any advice.'

Boase stayed at the Bartlett's until midnight. Caroline went to bed at just after ten o'clock and the two men sat with Topper, drinking and discussing what could be done about the whole dreadful situation.

Chapter Five

Superintendent Bolton stood with his back to the window in the main lobby of Falmouth Police Station. When his full team of police officers were assembled he locked the front door.

'Gentlemen. Things have taken a turn for the worse and we are in danger of having complaints lodged against us here at the station. That is not something I desire. I know you are all working hard in connection with your normal duties as well as the more recent events that have overtaken the usual routine, however, there have been new and unpleasant developments over the weekend.'

The assembled group looked around the room at each other; some of them had heard the latest, others not.

'For those of you who do not yet know, there was an incident aboard the Mermaid on Friday night; several people were taken ill with, sadly, another death due to poisoning.'

Superintendent Bolton did not normally look so strained but Boase could see in his face that the senior officer was now facing a struggle. Boase had heard the news on Saturday and had been called in to work on Sunday to work out a more efficient strategy. Superintendent Bolton had been very kind and not berated Boase for his efforts but made it quite clear that they had to see an end to this business before anything worse happened.

'The people affected and currently being treated at the hospital are as follows: Mr Arthur Nancarrow, Mrs Dorothy

Cornelius, The Honourable Edward Smythe and one death, that is Miss Topsy Beaufort. So you can see, gentlemen, if your gloves were indeed ever on, they must now be well and truly off. There is not a moment to waste. Constable Boase will be in charge of this, under my direction. If you have any questions, please ask either of us. There is absolutely no more time to waste. I will be having a meeting with Boase now in my office for the next half an hour. I suggest you get a cup of tea and stand by for orders. There will be no cutting corners, any breaks you have booked, unless compassionate or urgent will be cancelled for the foreseeable and I need your total commitment. Rabone, unlock that door please.'

Dr Masters looked at Archie Boase across the desk in his consulting room.

'Constable Boase – this is a terrible situation, illness, fatalities – they are all coming here and we are running out of beds. I know that's not important in the grand scheme, but if this continues, I really do not know what we shall do.'

'Yes, I understand Doctor. The four people from the Mermaid…all the same as before – thallium?'

'Yes, it looks that way – I'm awaiting the official report but there's no doubt in my mind.'

'How bad are the three? Are they as bad as Irene? Has their sight gone?'

'Two will be all right, the other, quite bad. It depends on how much of the poison they ingested that evening. But I can only do my job – if you and your colleagues could now do yours, mine would become easier. I'm sorry if that sounds flippant – but we really can't allow this to happen again. You need to find out who is doing this and stop them.'

'Yes, I know, Doctor. May I please look in on Irene as I'm here?'

'I'm sorry – the nurse is with her at the moment. But come back another time if you wish.'

'I will. Thank you.'

Boase returned to the station and to his desk. He found a pork pie in the drawer and he unwrapped it. He took his penknife and cut the pie into two pieces then went in search of tea. As he went into the lobby, Constable Penhaligon was drinking a cup of tea and chatting with Constables Coad and Eddy.

'Haven't you got any work to do? You're making me look bad. Where's Rabone?'

Penhaligon put down the cup.

'He's gone to see about a handbag theft. Sorry.'

'Never mind sorry – I'm going down to the Mermaid in a minute – Eddy, Coad…you come with me. Penhaligon, find something to do, and when Rabone returns, get your thinking caps on – I need all the help I can get.'

He looked at the two other constables.

'Be ready in fifteen minutes.'

Boase fetched his tea and sat eating his pork pie. He hated speaking to the others like that – others of his own rank, but that was Bolton's choice and he had told them so. Besides, if they were slacking, it made him look bad.

The three arrived at the Prince of Wales Pier where the Mermaid had remained since the events of Friday evening. No one had been permitted access since that night. Boase wandered over to Binny Vivian who was sitting on the steps mending a fishing net.

'Binny – who is in charge of the Mermaid these days?'

The old man looked up.

'Oh, 'ello, Constable Boase. You all right?'

'I've been better. Who is in charge of it?'

'It's Leslie Pentecost. Think 'e only bought it recently – don't know 'ow he afforded it. They say it's proper swanky now.'

'So where can I find him – any idea?'

'I think 'e went over to the Kimberley for a drink.'

'Thanks, Binny – come on you two.'

Boase pushed open the door of the Kimberley public bar and motioned to the two constables to pass through. The three went to the bar where a tall man around the age of forty stood cleaning some glasses. He looked up as they approached.

'What now? I don't want no trouble in 'ere.'

'There will be no trouble, Sir.'

Boase recognised William Parsons – he remembered him now of old and thought to himself how singular that an alcoholic had been given custody of a public house.

'There will be no trouble, Mr Parsons. Is Leslie Pentecost in here?'

William Parsons nodded towards a table in the corner by the window. Boase looked over and saw a man sitting with his feet up on a chair and reading a newspaper. He walked over to him. The man didn't look up.

'Leslie Pentecost?'

'What do you want?'

Boase introduced himself and the two constables.

'I need to talk to you about what happened aboard the Mermaid on Friday night.'

'Oh. Well, as it 'appens, I'd quite like to talk to you too. Pull up a pew.'

The three men sat and listened.

'What I want to know, Constable, is this. I 'eard that this isn't the first time local people have bin poisoned recently?'

'Yes, Sir, I'm afraid you are correct.'

'So, if you 'ad been doing your job, my customers would still be all right. And that poor, lovely woman dead too.'

Boase raised his voice and Coad and Eddy looked at each other in surprise. This was unusual for Boase to lose his patience with a member of the public.

'Mr Pentecost, if you don't mind, I am here to ask you questions – not the other way about. If you don't want to help me then it's only a short walk to the station and we can talk there?'

'All right, all right – keep your shirt on. Ask…'

'I want you to tell me what happened on Friday – did you see anything that looked suspicious, or anyone…especially where the food was concerned?'

'I can't say that I did. Everyone was enjoying themselves as they always do. Then at about nine o'clock, during the dinner, people started to complain they felt unwell, saying they felt sick.'

'What did you do?'

'Well, nothing at first. The water was getting a little rougher than usual so I just thought it was a bit of seasickness. Then, one or two got really bad and, well, you know the rest.'

'Do you have a list of the people on board the Mermaid that evening? And I'll need to see the menu and the galley.'

'Yes, but the menu is on the boat. You can come with me and I'll let you 'ave it if you think it'll 'elp. I just want this sorted…it will do no end of 'arm to me business and I 'aven't long started it up.'

'I understand that, Mr Pentecost, but at the moment there are rather more pressing matters to consider.'

Boase sent the two constables back to the station with further instructions. It had become apparent that this wasn't a three-man job. He couldn't even get that right. How useless he felt – and how he wished for George Bartlett's guidance.

Boase and the boat owner took the short walk to the Mermaid and went aboard. Leslie Pentecost handed Boase a menu from the Friday evening.

'Can I keep this?'

'elp yourself. I just hope you find out what's going on – I can't afford to lose money or for people to think that I 'ad something to do with this.'

'Why would they?'

'You know what people are like, Constable – small, mean-minded, nasty. You know how they'll be gossiping about this. And about you, yes, they'll be 'aving a field day with this little lot.'

'Thanks for your help – keep that boat secure and I'll be back again if I need to see you.'

Boase took an early break for his lunch and walked up to the Bartlett house. George Bartlett saw him from the window and came to open the front door.

'Hello, my boy. This is an unexpected visit at midday? What's happened? Come on in.'

Bartlett boiled the kettle and Boase stood with him in the scullery.

'I'm not coping, Sir.'

'What's that? Not coping? Of course you are. You're an expert in what you do – I've never doubted that for one minute. Come on, have some tea and tell me all about it.'

The pair sat in the parlour. Bartlett lit his pipe.

'Come on then. Let's have it, Boase.

'Bolton is expecting too much. It's more than I can do. He's put me in charge and I'm not man enough for the job.'

'Yes you are. What's particularly troubling you?'

'Well on top of all my worries about the poisonings – and, of course, about Irene, well Dr Cook came into the station yesterday. Remember Dr Cook, Sir?'

'Of course I remember him – and all that terrible business we went through with him. That was a bad case, indeed it was. What did he want?'

'Well, he reported that someone has attempted to end a woman's pregnancy – up in Well Lane.'

'Oh, right. Yes, we had this many times in London…'

'…but, Sir, the woman is dead.'

'Oh, my Lord. Oh, no. Who is it?'

'A woman called Marjorie Medlin.'

'What? I know her! She used to help Caroline with her charity arrangements. Oh, my. She was such a lovely woman. Caroline will be distraught. Oh! How terrible.'

'So, you see, Sir. I'm in a bit of a bind. I don't know which way to turn with it all.'

'Well, coincidentally, I have too much time on my hands – and we have been known before to break one or two small rules, have we not, my boy?'

'Well, yes, I s'pose.'

'So, how about letting me help you? Strictly off the record, of course – not a word to anyone.'

'Would you? Would you really do that for me, Sir?'

'I'm doing it for both of us. At this rate of boredom, I'll be up Bodmin in a minute.'

Boase laughed at George Bartlett's allusion to the lunatic asylum in that town.

'I would be so grateful, Sir. You see, I'm so worried this abortion business is going to fall to me too and I just can't deal with it all.'

'Calm down now. First things first. Have you been asked to deal with this business?'

'No. Not yet.'

'Well, then, no point worrying about it until it happens. Let's get on with this other business. I'll need to know as much as you can tell me. Anyway, look at the time – cut along back to work. How about you come back this evening? Have a bit of supper with us. It'll take Caroline out of herself a bit and then we can talk. Let's say about seven?'

'Seven will be perfect. Thank you. I'll see you then.'

Boase left the Bartlett house feeling like a weight had been lifted. George Bartlett would soon help him sort this. But, no one must find out or there would be trouble all round.

Edgar Villiers sat by his wife's bed. He cried.

'Eunice, my dear. I'm so sorry. I've been such a bad person, such a bad husband. I wish I could explain, but...but no one would understand. I loved you so much. I've always loved you. I love you now. But I couldn't deal with the way things turned out. I was bad – but you did a bad thing too. I wanted to forgive you but even when it was all over, I couldn't. You did a terrible thing. Before I knew it you ended up in here. I didn't plan that for you – I thought you were stronger than that. Maybe I wanted you to face up to what you had done, but instead, you crumbled and this was the only place for you...if you could only see...'

Edgar was interrupted by the Matron entering the room.

'Mr Villiers, Sir. It's almost half past. Your wife is very tired and she needs her medicine.'

Edgar kissed his wife's hand and left the room. Walking down the staircase he remembered the last time he had been here. As he left by the large oak front door, he looked across the garden to his motorcar. Topsy had been waiting for him then. Now he would ever see her again. He got into the driving seat, started the engine and drove off at top speed.

Boase walked into his office feeling a bit more at ease; he had spent the evening with George Bartlett – his friend, his mentor, his adviser. Bartlett had agreed to help and the two men had sat up late talking about everything that had gone on in recent weeks. Bartlett had offered guidance and advice and Boase had promised regular updates.

As Boase pulled open his desk drawer looking for food, the door opened and Superintendent Bolton came in.

'Good morning, Boase…you well?'

Boase slammed the drawer shut dreading what was coming next.

'Good morning, Sir. Yes, I'm well.'

'Boase, about this reported abortion…'

Boase's shoulders slumped.

'…I've decided, you have too much on your plate and it wouldn't be fair of me to ask you to take on this as well – so, I've decided to deal with this one myself. I know it's somewhat unorthodox but, well, in the absence of any further help from outside – and there are no signs of that yet – I think the best plan would be for me to take this on.'

Boase couldn't have agreed more but didn't let his relief show.

'Well, Sir – if you're sure. I mean…I don't mind…'

'No, you just carry on with the poisonings and try to put all that to bed. Leave the rest to me.'

Bolton left the office, quietly shutting the door behind him. Boase was grateful that he wasn't on at him all the time; that must mean that he trusted him to be left alone. That, he felt, was a compliment.

Boase had listened to what Bartlett had said the evening before and the older man's advice was to go back to the beginning; revisit past events. He had suggested going to the three sites where the poisonings appeared to be the source and try to find a link – and to be vigilant; anything, however small, could be a clue. With this in mind, Boase took Constable Eddy and the pair made their way to George's café.

'Mrs Tremayne, how long have you been cook here at George's?'

Mrs Tremayne stood with her hands on her large hips and thought.

'Well now, let me just think a minute. I 'aven't always been cook, mind. I started 'ere as a waitress in, let me see, yes, that's right nineteen hundred and six, so I bin 'ere nigh on twenty years. Cook? I became cook when Mr Dudley took bad, 'e was a lovely man – trained in Paris I do believe. Very good 'e was. Made the tiniest little pastry things, fit for the King 'imself we used to say. Anyway, where was I? Oh, right, yes. Mr Dudley was took bad. One minute 'e was 'is usual self – making little apple tarts 'e was, right where you're standing now, young man.'

Constable Eddy fidgeted on the spot as Mrs Tremayne gestured towards him.

'Yes – right there, I can see 'im as if it was yesterday. My, such a lovely man, always 'appy. Alive right up till 'e died 'e was.'

Boase concealed a grin at this point, not quite knowing what to make of that comment.

'So, Mrs Tremayne, can you give me any thoughts on what might have happened when the Laitys came in here to eat? Can you tell me anything at all that might be relevant? And of course, we need to look in your pantry, if that's all right?'

'You look where you like, young man. But I can't think what could 'ave made 'im ill. I know they say it's some sort of poison but, well, no one else 'as been took bad since. And, as you know, we 'ad your people in 'ere looking at all the food – we was closed for two days while they looked at everything.'

'Yes, I know – they were from up country, experts in that sort of thing. But what I don't understand is, if they're so expert, why didn't they find anything here? Mrs Tremayne, is it possible that Mr Laity brought something of his own to eat onto the premises?'

'I don't know…but…'

'… but what?'

Mrs Tremayne looked thoughtful for a moment.

'What is it? Have you remembered something? Please, think!'

'Well, there is something – I don't know if they looked at it…Gentleman's Relish they call it.'

'What? What do you mean?'

'Mr Laity asked for the condiment tray – both times 'e was in 'ere. Gentleman's Relish. The first time, 'e tried it and said it was very nice. The second time 'e 'ad it and said it wasn't up to much. I thought it might be off – I'd never seen it before. I didn't like the smell of it if I'm 'onest…so I didn't put it on the tray again. I do believe that 'e was the only person to 'ave that. Oh my! Did I kill 'im, Constable? Did *I* kill Mr Laity?'

'No, Mrs Tremayne. Of course you didn't. Do you still have this condiment?'

'Yes. It's in the pantry – it seemed such a waste to throw it away, even though it didn't smell too good.'

'Show me.'

Mrs Tremayne obliged and handed the ceramic jar to Boase. He opened the lid and sniffed.'

'Well, I agree – it smells horrible. Are you sure Mr Laity was the only person to eat this?'

'I can't be absolutely sure, but I think so. I always make up the trays and so none of the other girls would think about putting it back out. I filled a little pot of it and gave it to 'im with his food.'

'I need to take this away, Mrs Tremayne.'

'Am I in trouble, Constable?'

The cook looked worried.

'Absolutely not – if I had a medal, I'd give it to you. Thank you so much.'

Boase felt encouraged with his find in Mrs Tremayne's pantry. So, if Percy Laity was the only person to eat this condiment, then that could be the source of the poison. He began to feel as though Bartlett was working alongside him now, spurring him on. He would get this pot of relish examined and then do a more thorough search of the other establishments…especially the one that had hurt his beloved girl. Yes, that would be his next stop, the Rose Tearooms. All he knew was that Irene's chocolates were purchased there. She had offered some to her parents but they didn't like Turkish Delight. He returned to the police station to arrange for the relish to be scrutinised. Yes, the experts had been called in but had failed to detect this. As Boase placed the small ceramic pot on his desk, he resolved to sort this out, for Irene and for her father. He would make them proud. No more self-doubt.

Chapter Six

Alice Hole, a timid young woman probably in her thirties, sat on the seat in the Falmouth police station lobby. She pulled her shawl around her shoulders and looked at the floor. The desk sergeant approached her.

'Can I help you, Madam?'

Alice coughed and stood up.

'I need to see someone, Sir.'

'Can I ask what it's about?'

Alice looked about her nervously and tightened her shawl still further. She lowered her voice.

'It's about, umm…it's about that lady. Mrs Medlin. I know something. The lady that died.'

'What's your name?'

'My name is Alice Hole, Sir.'

'Come with me please, Madam.'

The desk sergeant led her to Superintendent Bolton's door, knocked and waited for the familiar voice to bid him enter.

'Sir, sorry to interrupt, Sir…this lady is Alice Hole. I think you might like to talk to her – it's about Mrs Medlin.'

'Please come in, Mrs Hole – is it Mrs?'

'Yes, Sir. Mrs Alice Hole – but please call me Alice.'

'Have a seat, Alice. Would you like some tea?'

'No, thank you, Sir.'

'So, what do you want to speak about?'

'It's about Mrs Medlin. I know what happened to her.'

'What do you mean?'

'I know about the baby. I knew Marjorie Medlin and she told me about the baby. Told me she didn't know how she would be able to feed another, although to me they always seemed quite comfortably off. Said her husband would be furious if he found out. I reminded her that it was as much him that got her in that way as she. She said to me she knew someone that could help – you know what I mean, Sir?'

'Yes, Alice, I know what you mean.'

'I told her straight. "Marjorie,' I said, 'you mustn't go doing anything bad. Never. A baby is always a blessing, a gift from God." No, she wouldn't have it. She'd made up her mind.'

'Can I ask, how did you know Mrs Medlin?'

'Oh, we're near neighbours. I've known her for over twenty years. That's how I saw what I saw that day.'

'Please, Alice, tell me what you know – what you saw.'

'I don't need to tell you, Sir. I can show you.'

Superintendent Bolton looked on, puzzled as Alice Hole delved deep into her bag. She withdrew a piece of paper, slightly bigger than postcard sized. She pushed it across the desk and the Superintendent looked more puzzled still.

'I'm sorry, I don't understand. What is this?'

He regarded the paper with the powerfully drawn sketch; a skilful image of a woman was staring back at him from the paper.

'I think that's her. That's the woman who killed Marjorie.'

'Did you draw this, Alice?'

'Yes, Sir. I did. I always wanted to be an artist but, well, that was never going to be possible – but I still draw and paint when I can…and that's her. That's the image of the woman who killed Marjorie Medlin.

Superintendent Bolton leaned back in his chair.

'Alice, that's a very serious accusation you've just made.'

'I know, Sir. But, Marjorie didn't deserve that – and I stand by what I say.'

'May I please keep this sketch? It's very good – is it a good likeness of the woman you saw?'

'It's as good as any photograph, Sir.'

'Thank you. Just let me make a note of the times you say you saw this woman and then you can go. And you actually saw her go into the house – and leave again?'

'Yes, Sir. I did. I'm not a busybody but that day I wasn't feeling too good so I drew a chair up to the parlour window, lit the fire and made myself a hot drink. From the window I can see across the street to Marjorie's house – the scullery door is at the side of the house, that's where she went in and came out.'

'Thank you – I hope this will help with our investigations. Please leave your address with the desk sergeant in case we need to speak to you again.'

'Yes, I will. Good bye.'

Superintendent Bolton looked again at the sketch and thought what a talented woman Alice was.

Archie Boase sat in the Bartlett's parlour and listened to George and Caroline. They had just come from the hospital.

'Look my boy, as they say, there's good news and there's bad news. The good news is that when we visited Irene this afternoon, she woke up. She heard her mother talking to her and she woke up – after all this time!'

'That's such good news, Sir. Can I see her again soon?'

'Yes, I'm sure you can but, wait, there's more. She couldn't see anything. She's blind.'

'Oh, dear God. Please no. Will she see again?'

'They don't see how it's possible, although it has been known to happen before where people have suffered some sort of temporary blindness – then regained their sight. But I have to tell you, they're not confident for our Irene.'

Caroline placed her hand on her husband's arm.

'George, dear. Where there's life, there's hope. You know that's true. Archie, we all have to pray hard now for Irene and hope for her sight to be restored.'

'Mrs Bartlett, I'm sorry – but if God existed, why would he do this to our beautiful girl? Why would he be so damned cruel?!'

'Boase, control yourself, control your language.'

'I'm so sorry.'

'It's all right, my boy – you're only saying what I was thinking. And I know what you've seen in France and why you might have lost faith. But Caroline is right – where there's life there's hope and, well, God has seen fit not to take her from us and for that we must be glad.'

'I know, Sir. I'm sorry.'

'Don't be sorry. Why don't you go and look in on her tomorrow? She asked for you.'

'She asked for me? Really? Oh! What did she say?'

Caroline looked across the room at Boase.

'She said "where's my Archie?" That's what she said.'

'I can't wait to talk to her.'

Dolly Combellack laid her knitting down in her lap and looked at the clock. It was almost half past ten in the evening. She listened. She could hear voices in the next house. Louder and louder now. She listened again, yes, two women. Now a man joined the argument. The terraced houses that ascended Killigrew Street were solidly built but even their walls were no match for the occupants this night. A scratching at the scullery door caused Dolly to leave her armchair and open the door to the small back garden. The old lady bent down and scooped up Fancy, the little tabby cat who had voluntarily moved in with Dolly two years previously and now showed no signs of moving out again. Dolly, twenty-seven years a widow, was happy with this arrangement and glad of Fancy's company.

'Come in, Fancy. Come in my lovely. Mother has a little bit of fish for you. Come on in.'

The cat jumped from Dolly's arms and ran into the scullery. Dolly paused and listened. Her neighbours had opened their back door and the argument continued. As Dolly turned to go inside, she couldn't help but overhear the man's voice again.

'I warned you, my girl. Don't bring no trouble 'ome 'ere. And look what you've done. I've warned you, yer mother's warned you. Why couldn't you be a good girl like yer sisters? I don't know what'll become of you – you can't stay 'ere no more. Sixteen years old. *Sixteen!* And if you don't tell me who did this, I'll take my belt off and I'll beat it out of you.'

At that point, there was a loud crash and a woman's scream. Dolly hurried inside and bolted the scullery door.

Boase arrived at the station at seven o'clock the next morning. He felt stronger now. He was going to see Irene later on. He had been up late trying to find something decent to wear, he wanted to look nice for his girl; he knew she couldn't see him at the moment but he would feel better. Irene always liked him to look nice. Superintendent Bolton had afforded him the luxury of uniform or mufti, his choice, and he had chosen the latter since he had become accustomed to this when he had worked with George Bartlett. So, today Archie Boase wore the dark navy suit that was Irene's favourite. She had told him how handsome he had looked in it. He'd shaved late last night and again this morning – Irene hated a man who had a rough beard – and, she might just touch his cheek and, how awful! If the love of his life touched his cheek and it was rough.

Boase spent the early part of the morning taking advice and instructions from Superintendent Bolton and then made ready to visit the Rose Tearooms and the Mermaid. He now realised, after his visit to George's Café, that the so called experts had not done their job very thoroughly at all by overlooking the Gentleman's Relish and returning a clean bill of health for the kitchen at George's. After his initial uncertainty and now galvanised by George Bartlett's input and the chance to maybe speak to Irene, Boase was ready to deal with all of this now. People in authority were trusting him and this might be his chance to stand out, to shine. And if he stood out there might be better things ahead and a way to give Irene what she would need when she eventually came to him.

With Constable Rabone at his side, Boase took the short walk up to High Street and to the Rose Tearooms. They had just opened for mid-morning teas. The two men entered and a young waitress approached them.

'Good morning, gentlemen, can I get you a table?'

No, thank you, Miss. My name is Constable Boase and I would like to speak to the manager if I could.'

'Wait a minute, please. I'll fetch him – it's Mr Simpson'

Boase and Rabone waited, peering into the wooden cabinets at the various confectionery treats until they were interrupted.

'How can I help you, gentlemen?'

A tall, middle-aged man stood between them. Despite his above average height he still had a sort of hunchback and he swayed to one side as he walked. Boase scowled as he caught sight of Rabone staring, and introduced them both.

'Sir, as the manager, you no doubt remember our associates coming to examine your premises in the aftermath of at least one of your customers being poisoned?'

'Yes, yes I do – but we can hardly be blamed for that now, can we?'

'No, no one is blaming you, Sir, but we do have a duty to fully investigate, particularly as we could now be dealing with a murder enquiry through an episode at another establishment.'

'Oh. Oh dear me. How terrible. How can I help you?'

'I want to look over everything again and maybe speak to your staff to see if they might remember anything in particular that could help us. I also want a list of people who supply you with your food. Can you provide that?'

'Yes, of course I can. I will also arrange for you to speak with the staff if you think that might help. Here you are, maybe you'd like to start with Florence?'

'Florence was the waitress who had welcomed Boase and Rabone when they arrived. Mr Simpson gave them permission to use his upstairs office for their interviews and the three sat in the window looking across the water to Flushing.

'Florence, can you tell us anything you know that might help? Anything unusual – any unusual people that you don't normally see?'

'I don't think so, Sir. Not really – only…'

'…only what, Florence?'

'Well, just that strange man that came in here a few weeks ago trying to sell us stuff.'

'What – you mean a commercial traveller?'

'I suppose so – but he was a bit strange I thought.'

'In what way?'

'Well, he looked a bit nervous, usually those types have the gift of the gab if you know what I mean – trying to get you to buy more and more stuff. I know because Mr Simpson always asks us girls what we think so that we know what we're giving to our customers. But he seemed strange – he didn't look like they usually do, I suppose.

'Florence, this is so very important. Please think harder. Can you tell me what was purchased from him?'

'Yes, I can tell you that. It was boxes of chocolates. Like the ones we have downstairs in the cabinet – you walked past them when you came in.'

'Do you still have them?'

Boase with Rabone and Florence descended the stairs to the lobby just as Mr Simpson came from behind the desk.

'Mr Simpson, please be so good as to unlock these cabinets, I'm afraid I will have to take away all this stock for examination.'

'You can't be serious, Constable?'

'I'm very serious – I believe that these chocolates may have been contaminated with poison.'

'But we've sold several with no ill-effect.'

'That's as maybe, Sir, but at least one of your customers has suffered very ill-effects and I mean to find out what has happened. Your establishment may well become the source of another poisoning incident. Please unlock the cabinets.'

Mr Simpson, now looking rather pale, obliged, and packed about two dozen boxes of chocolates into suitable containers for Boase and Rabone to carry. The two men left, retracing their steps back down High Street.

'What do you think, Rabone? Reckon there's anything in these boxes that shouldn't be?'

'What, like thallium?'

'Exactly. Inspector Bartlett has told me that Irene dined here that evening, eating similar food to several other diners. However, she did take away a box of Turkish Delight – just like we have here. It's her favourite. My God! If I catch whoever has been doing this…'

The two reached the station and presented their findings to Superintendent Bolton.

'Well done, Boase – I'm sorry you've had to go over old ground but, good work. This should have been picked up by the experts that came to analyse all this stuff. Seems to me that they weren't looking beyond the ends of their noses. You've done a good job, finding that Gentleman's Relish and now this confectionery. Very thorough work indeed. What's your next plan?'

'I think, Sir, the plan would be to return to the Mermaid and see if anything has been overlooked there? But I do have an urgent hospital visit on my way there, if that's all right, Sir?'

'Yes, of course – you're due a break. Hope your girl is on the mend. Well, I'll leave it to you then. I have a lead with the Medlin case and I'm keen to move on with that. Headquarters have sent me a spare man, I'm snowed under. Good work, Boase - Bartlett has obviously taught you well.'

Boase couldn't wait to get out and on his way to the hospital. He couldn't wait to see Irene. He stopped at the florist's and bought a bunch of the strongest smelling flowers in the shop. Irene loved flowers and if she couldn't see them, well, Boase wanted her to smell them. He rushed up Killigrew Street and made his way through the hospital to Irene's room. He stopped at the door. The room was empty. No bed. No Irene. In a panic he returned to the corridor just in time to see Phyll. He ran up to her.

'Hello, Archie. How nice to see you.'

'Where is she? Where's Irene?'

Phyll smiled and Boase couldn't help but look at her nose. No, it still didn't wrinkle.

'She's been moved to a ward – on account of she's slightly improved. Come with me, I'll show you.'

Boase followed the nurse to a ward with four beds. Irene was at the end by the window.

'Thanks, Phyll.'

'Pleasure.'

Boase hesitated. He could see the bottom of Irene's bed from behind a curtain. He walked across the room, his legs felt like lead. He paused by the curtain then, one more step and he was looking at her. She had her face towards the window and the sun was shining on her hair. Tears pricked his eyes. He laid the flowers on the bed and spoke softly.

'Irene. It's me. I've…I've come to see you.'

Irene turned her head towards him and she smiled.

'Archie. Oh! Archie – is it really you?'

'Yes, my lovely girl. It's me.'

Irene half sat up and put her arms up to him. He held her for a moment then lifted her higher onto the pillows.

'How are you, Archie?'

'I should be asking you that. Here, I've brought you some flowers. Smell these – all your favourites are here.'

He placed the flowers into Irene's hands and she held them up to her face. Boase thought how beautiful she looked – and that she might never be able to see herself in the mirror again.

'Thank you for coming. I'm sorry about everything.'

A tear fell onto Irene's nightgown.

'Please don't cry, Irene. I've missed you so much. It was all my fault. I've been such a clot. Can you ever forgive me?'

'There's nothing to forgive – we've been a pair of idiots, and now…well, now, I suppose it's over.'

'Irene – please don't say that. I had hoped there would be another chance for us.'

'Why would you want to be with a useless blind girl? Just get out now while you have the chance. Find someone else.'

'Irene, please don't – it's you, only you I've wanted all along. My dearest girl, I've never wanted anyone else – I only have eyes for you.'

'And now, I have eyes for no one.'

'Oh, Irene – I'm sorry – I didn't mean…'

'…see, see how awkward it's going to be?'

Irene turned once more to the window.

'It won't be. Just say you'll take me back – please, I can't live without you in my life. They say your sight may be restored one day, it's happened before. Irene, my darling girl – say you'll take me back. I can't live without you. You're my world.'

'You can't spend your life with a blind woman, Archie. It wouldn't be fair.'

'But maybe I want to take care of you – I love you so much, Irene – don't do this to us. Please, I'm begging you.'

Boase took Irene's small hand in his and kissed it.

'Look, Irene, I have work – I'm trying to find out who did this to you. But, please don't let me leave hopeless. Please say there's a chance for us?'

'Will you come to see me again, Archie?'

'Of course – if that's all right with you. I'd love to.'

Boase leaned forward and kissed Irene's head and then her cheek.

'I'll come back very soon – and hopefully in a while I'll be able to take you out of here with me. Good bye, my love.'

'Goodbye, Archie – and thank you.'

Chapter Seven

Superintendent Bolton looked at the sketch given to him by Alice Hole. What now? What should he do next? As he continued to look and wonder, a knock at the door followed by it being pushed open signalled the return of Boase.

'I'm back, Sir. Just to let you know.'

'Come in a moment, Boase, will you? How's Irene?'

'Well, better than she was thanks, Sir. But she can't see and it's distressing her.'

'It's bound to. Will she see again?'

'Maybe – but they can't say. I remember how the men in France felt when they realised they were blind…I think that was one of the most terrifying disabilities – knowing that you would never see again. And Irene, well, I don't know if she'll cope.'

'I know, Boase, but the fact is, she'll have to. She'll get through – especially with you by her side.'

'I hope so, Sir.'

Boase, can I ask you about this?'

The older man showed Boase the sketch.

'Do you know that woman?'

'No, I don't think so…should I?'

'Apparently she could be our abortionist.'

'Oh – how so?'

'A woman named Alice Hole, nice woman, came in with this. She's a neighbour of Marjorie Medlin and she said this is the woman she saw going into and leaving the house at the time this all appeared to happen. I think we have to take it seriously – and in the absence of anything else.'

'Well, I can ask around if that might help…'

'…you have such a lot on, but maybe we could get a copy and you could take it about with you, just in case.'

'Yes, I can do that – you never know. Someone might know something. Let's get a copy then, if we can.'

'Thanks, Boase.'

'I've just got time to go back to the Mermaid now, Sir. Be interesting to see if anything has been overlooked there too.'

'Yes, well, I wish you luck with that.'

Boase and Rabone took the short walk to the Mermaid and went aboard. 'Leslie Pentecost was not to be found which suited Boase. The pair went into the galley.

'Right, Rabone, you know the drill – look for anything suspicious in the cupboards – there shouldn't be any food left here but this is the one eaterie that hasn't returned us any results yet. So what we know is that the Rose Tearooms returned nothing but they didn't analyse the chocolates, George's Café returned nothing but they didn't analyse the Gentleman's Relish. So, here we're awaiting the results but after the other two, I don't really trust them too much – they could cost me the case with their slackness.'

'But, how will I now if the food has poison in?'

Boase scowled at Rabone.'

'Well, you could taste it?'

'But it might be poisonous…'

'…I was joking, you fool. You won't know, but if anything is still left here we need to take it away. It really is that simple, Rabone. Anyway, you know what they say…'

'No - what?'

'The proof of the pudding…'

Boase laughed out loud at his own comment and Rabone ignored him.

The two men scoured the cupboards from top to bottom. Not one item of food remained. They searched again to be sure but there was nothing.

'Looks like they were a bit more thorough here – but, then again, it's a much smaller premises to search. Right, Rabone, let's call it a day.

The weather took a turn for the worse that evening. Caroline Bartlett sat up in bed. She had those chest pains again. She thought she had begun to feel better but now, all this business with Irene, well, she didn't feel well at all now. She hadn't told her husband but, after so many years of marriage, he knew. They knew each other inside out. She reached for her pills in the dark but tipped over the small glass of water she had brought up to bed with her. It fell to the floor. George Bartlett sat upright, wide awake.

'Princess...what are you doing?'

'I'm trying to be quiet, dear.'

'Not successfully – let me help you, you can't do that in the dark.'

'I didn't want to wake you.'

Bartlett lit the room and went downstairs to fetch a cloth and some more water. He returned with Topper following behind.

'The boy's worried about you, seems you woke him up too. Here she is, old man. Look, she's all right. Have you got your pills now? Why didn't you tell me you felt unwell?'

'It's just a little pain, George, nothing really.'

'You must stop worrying about everything – you worry if you have nothing to worry about. Now, come on, back to bed, it's almost three o'clock.'

'Sorry, George.'

Topper lay by Caroline's side of the bed and looked up at her.

'Can he stay, dear?'

'Yes – but you shouldn't keep spoiling him.'

'That's good, coming from you. He's just worried, let him be.'

The light went out and all three occupants at the Bartlett household settled down again.

The three Bartletts lay in the darkness trying to find sleep again. After about twenty minutes, George turned and looked at Caroline.

'Princess, you still awake?'

No reply came. He was glad she had managed to fall asleep, she had been so tired and looked strained with everything that was happening lately. He smiled as he heard Topper gently snoring. Suddenly there was a noise at the front door. Bartlett jumped up out of bed and ran to the window, tripping over Topper who let out a yelp.

'What the...?!'

As Bartlett peered through the window, he saw a figure leaving the front garden. He heard the gate swing shut and the figure was gone. Bartlett ran downstairs and pulled something from the letter box. He fetched his reading spectacles from the parlour and examined the piece of paper under the hallway lamp. He read the following:

Mr Bartlett, I know you are no longer involved with the police but I just needed to get something off my chest. I am your poisoner. I can't tell you my name but I have a very good reason for doing what I've done.

Will I strike again? Maybe.

Bartlett sank down onto the bottom stair. Who is this? Why is it being sent to him? He sat for about ten minutes then went into the scullery to make some tea. He looked several times more at the note while he was waiting for the kettle to boil. It didn't make any sense. More disconcerting still, this man knew him and where he lived – so he knew where Irene lived too. What was going on? He drank some tea and went back up to bed but he couldn't sleep. This was a preposterous situation and one he was unsure how to deal with. He should at the very least show this to Boase – now that it was his case.

Boase sat at his desk and searched the drawers. Empty. No food. He was sure he had left a piece of Mrs Curgenven's fruit cake in there. He went to the front desk and looked at the sergeant who was leaning on the desk reading the Falmouth Packet. He hurriedly folded it and threw it on the table behind him.

'It's okay – don't worry. I just came in search of food. Got any?'

The desk sergeant grinned. He had never known anyone with such an appetite.

'I might just have one or two biscuits in my tin.'

He reached beneath the desk.

'Ohh…did your wife make them? Are they those little ones with currants in?'

'The very same…look.'

The sergeant opened the tin and held them in front of Boase.

'Well, you're not supposed eat on the front desk, you know. But I won't tell anyone if…'

'Here – there are three left. Take them…I'm fat enough and you're as skinny as a rake. There's no justice in this world.'

Boase took the biscuits and returned to his office.

Four days passed and absolutely nothing had happened to further either the poisoning or the abortion cases. Boase didn't like this state of limbo. He sat at his desk and re-read his evidence list; it was very short. Superintendent Bolton came into the room.

'Good morning, Boase. I've just got the food analysis results back that you requested. I haven't opened it – thought you might like to.'

Bolton handed Boase the envelope.

'Thank you, Sir. Blimey, I'm worried now.'

'Just open it – my fingers are crossed.'

Boase tore open the brown envelope and looked at the report. '

'Well? Any luck?'

'Yes, Sir. Absolutely. Chocolates from the Rose Tearooms have thallium, Gentleman's Relish from George's Café also thallium. And it's got the original request from the Mermaid too. Tartare sauce – thallium. Oh my word! No wonder so many people were ill – apparently everyone asks for that on the boat when they have fish.'

'Indeed. What now, Boase?'

Well, the waitress at the Rose Tearooms said the chocolates were bought from a commercial traveller who hadn't supplied them before – if I could link him in with George's and the Mermaid then we might be getting somewhere.'

'Yes, but even so, you'd still have to find him.'

'I know, there's the rub, Sir. But, I've got somewhere to start from now which is what I was hoping for.'

'You've done well, Boase – I have every faith in you. Oh, by the way, I nearly forgot, here's the copy of that picture I promised. Maybe your luck will continue with her too.'

'I'll do my best, Sir.'

'I know you will. I'll leave you to it then.'

Boase looked at the clock – it was just after midday. The morning had passed uneventfully but he had been encouraged to discover that all three establishments had apparently been sold poisonous food. He now needed to check if George's Café and the Mermaid had encountered the same man that the waitress had described to him - he desperately hoped this would be the case – but then, as Superintendent Bolton had pointed out, he had to find the man. Not only that, what if it wasn't to do with the traveller and someone else had tampered with the food? That didn't even bear thinking about. No, for now, Boase would follow this line.

Hunger once more getting the better of him, Boase went out into the street, crossed the Moor and headed to Belman's bakery. Jacob Belman was deemed to be the best baker in Cornwall and the people of Falmouth liked nothing more than the Jewish delights that came from his shop. Boase was after cake and Jacob Belman did not disappoint. As Boase left the shop clutching his paper bag of delights, he almost knocked over George Bartlett who was making his way into the shop.

'Look where you're going, Boase, you almost had me over!'

'Oh, I'm so sorry, Sir. I didn't see you.'

'Obviously.'

Bartlett grinned, pleased to see the younger man.

'Aren't you working?'

'Yes, but I was hungry and fancied a couple of cakes.'

'Well, you've come to the best place. Do you know, when I was a young man, all over the East End of London you could smell the wonderful Jewish bakeries every morning. Yes, that takes me right back. There are no better bakers, Boase, let me tell you. And, my! Aren't we lucky to have Mr Belman right on our doorstep?'

'Yes, indeed.'

Actually, Boase, when I've got Caroline's loaf, do you have a minute or two spare?'

'Well, I really ought to get back…'

…'it's work related.'

'Well, in that case, yes, of course. I'll wait here for you.'

Bartlett bought the loaf and the two men crossed the Moor and sat on a bench. Boase had already started on the first bun and pigeons welcomed the crumbs falling at his feet.

'What did you want me for, Sir?

Bartlett lit his pipe and recounted the story of the stranger in the garden and the note pushed through his front door. In return, Boase explained to Bartlett what had happened about the thallium results. He also told him about the sketch of the woman that Alice Hole had brought into the station.

'What shall I do next, Sir? I really need your help on this.'

'Well, if I were you, I'd first check if that commercial traveller sold those products to all three establishments – then I'd hunt him down.'

Boase chuckled.

'I don't think it'll be quite that easy, Sir.'

'Why not? You now have his handwriting, too.'

'But – do you really believe that's him? It could all be a hoax, couldn't it?'

'Well, you'll have to trust my instinct on this one, Boase. Got a feeling about it. I can't quite work it out – but I'll tell you when I do. Let me see this sketch anyway…got it with you?'

'Yes, here.'

Boase pulled the sketch from his pocket and gave it to Bartlett. The older man studied it for a moment then returned it.

'Doesn't ring any bells with me, but I'll keep a look out for you. They think she's the abortionist?'

'Apparently so.'

'This has happened before around here – but we never catch them. But I don't think we've ever had a death as a direct result. It's too bad, really too bad.'

The Falmouth Parish Church was full. The hearse bearing Topsy Beaufort's coffin stopped outside and four solemn figures carried her up the steps and into the church. Her mother and father were kneeling in the first pew in front of the altar. They stood as their daughter's coffin was placed right beside them. Mrs Beaufort lifted the black veil covering her face and dabbed her eyes with a white handkerchief which was edged with black. Brigadier Beaufort patted his wife's arm and whispered to her.

'Jacynth, please don't be sad. Topsy hated to see you cry.'

He turned around to check on his sons who were standing behind him. Davy, Carberry and Johnson Beaufort were staring at the coffin, barely believing that their sister was gone. She had been so full of life, had so many friends. No, they couldn't believe it; less than a month ago she was laughing with them at a card game, laughing because she had cheated them out of money and they had discovered her. But Topsy was Topsy – well, had been Topsy. Now the Beauforts would have to get used to life without her. The organ struck up and the congregation sang Abide with Me. As the vicar bid everyone to be seated, Carberry looked across the aisle. He nudged his brothers either side of him. They also looked across. There was Edgar Villiers. The source of so much stress to their mother and despised by the whole family. The Brigadier had tried to separate his young daughter from the older married man but, the harder he had tried, the more the headstrong girl had resisted.

'My dear people, it is with great sadness that I greet you here today in our beautiful church and in the presence of God. Brigadier and Mrs Beaufort have lost a beautiful – we have all lost a beautiful daughter and anyone who knew Patricia will know how she filled everyone's lives with love and laughter.'

At this point someone called out.

'Topsy – her name is Topsy!'

Everyone turned and looked at Edgar Villiers who had risen from his seat and was directly addressing the vicar. The three brothers looked at him with contempt.

'Well, yes, I know we are all in a high state of anxiety and upset…'

The vicar tried to continue. Edgar Villiers left his seat and stormed to the back of the church heading towards the door. He paused and turned back, facing the vicar on the altar.

'Damn your eyes! Damn and blast all of you!'

There was a communal gasp at this outburst, quickly followed by another, as the three Beaufort brothers rushed to the back of the church. They ran out into the street after Villiers but he had gone.

'He's probably gone up the steps.'

Johnson ran up behind the church and quickly returned to the other two men.

'Damned light on his feet for an old man.'

Davy kicked the wall in frustration.

'Well, that…that – old man shouldn't have been running round with our sister. How many times did Father warn him off? It's probably his fault she's dead.'

Johnson put his arm on Davy's shoulder.

'Don't be foolish – of course it's not his fault. As much as we hate him, I do believe he actually loved her. Come on now. Topsy wouldn't want us behaving like this, would she?'

Davy shrugged his brother's arm away and pushed back his auburn hair. Tears were pricking his eyes.

'Of course he didn't love her. Probably just wanted to get his hands on Father's money.'

Carberry intervened now.

'I think Edgar Villiers has plenty of money of his own…he comes from a shipping line on his mother's side and something wealthy on his father's you know. Why, I wouldn't be surprised if he didn't have more than Father. No, I don't think that's what he's about.'

'Well, I thought we three agreed – that we detested him. I've heard it's all his fault that his wife is in the mad house.'

'Enough now, come on, let's go back in – we're upsetting Mother and Father.

The three young men made their way back into the church, in time to join in with 'The Day Thou Gavest Lord Has Ended.'

Chapter Eight

'Mrs Jameson, if you want me to help you, you have to remain still.'

'I'm so sorry – I'm very nervous. Will everything be all right?'

'As long as you do as I say, it'll be all done and dusted in no time. Come on now, have a sip of your tea – I've put two sugars in. I'll have one as well, before I get properly started.'

The woman went downstairs and returned with a kettle of steaming hot water and a tin bowl from the scullery.

'Right now, dear, just lie back on the bed. You're quite late on, aren't you? This isn't going to be easy – but I've seen worse. Now, just relax.'

Edgar Villiers parked his car outside his house, having returned from a visit to his wife at Meadowbank. It was late and he felt bad because Eunice hadn't wanted him to leave. She had screamed and cried so much, interspersed with bouts of silence and staring, that the Matron had permitted him to stay on until all appeared calm again. As Villiers unlocked the front door and entered the hallway of his large house overlooking the river at Helford Passage, he was pushed to the floor and a sharp kick was delivered to his stomach. He groaned and tried to get up. As another kick came to his stomach, so another came to his back. Villiers tried to look up to see his attackers but there was no light. The moon was casting a small, golden beam through the side window but not enough to see anything by. As Villiers tried again to sit up, the assailants passed silently through the open front door and ran off down the drive. The injured man collapsed into unconsciousness.

Superintendent Bolton came into Boase's office.

'Any idea of what happened at Helford Passage last night, Boase?'

'No, Sir. Why? What have you heard?'

'Oh, apparently some well-to-do place was broken into…nothing stolen but the owner was turned over good and proper. I'm sorry, you have so much on – and I don't see this is related in any way to what we're working on, but could you have a look in later? The man is in hospital recovering but the village Bobby out at Mawnan Smith is complaining – says he won't be satisfied until someone from here takes a look at the house. Seems there have been about half a dozen burglaries in as many weeks but no one assaulted.'

This was the last thing Boase needed.

'Right o', Sir – I'll try and get out there this afternoon if that's all right?'

'Fine – thank you, Boase…and for all you're doing.'

'Pleasure, Sir.'

Boase bit into a huge slice of sponge cake with jam and cream in the middle. No, it wasn't a pleasure. Why did he even say that? Why did he always say that? It wasn't a pleasure – it was a flaming nuisance.

Boase, later that afternoon, thinking he could kill two birds with one stone, decided to visit the hospital to discover more if possible about the assault and, his main reason, to look in on Irene. He met a junior doctor on the way into the hospital, introduced himself, and announced his business there. The doctor led him to a side room. He pushed open the door and indicated to the seated nurse that the occupant of the room had a visitor. She stood as Boase entered.

'Please sit down, Nurse. How is he?'

'He's not good – but the doctor says he'll recover.'

'That's good news then. Can I speak to him?'

'He's just woken up and he's in and out as it were but, yes, you can talk. Would you like me to leave you?'

'If that would be all right, yes, thank you, Nurse.'

'Well, no more than ten minutes then please.'

'Ten minutes is more than enough, I'm sure.'

'Mr Villiers…'

Edgar Villiers turned his head and looked at Boase.

'Who are you?'

'I'm Constable Boase, Sir. I've come to just ask you if you have any idea what happened last night? Do you know who did this to you?'

Villiers wet his lips with his tongue.

'No…no I don't know. But there are plenty who wouldn't hesitate to get rid of me.'

'Why would you say that, Mr Villiers? Who are you thinking of – anyone in particular?'

'No – but I was chased out of the church at Topsy Beaufort's funeral – by her brothers. That family detests me. They think I'm a bounder, well I'm not. I loved that girl, really loved her. I've had threats from her father…'

'What sorts of threats?'

'Well…I dunno, but making it clear that I was not to see his daughter again – but she loved me too. The Brigadier turned the whole family against me. I would have married that girl tomorrow, Constable.'

'But, Sir, forgive me – aren't you already married?'

'Well, yes, yes, I am – but what I meant was…I was trying to explain how much I loved her.'

'So you have no idea who your attackers were? Could it have been the brothers? How many were there?'

'Two – I saw two. Maybe, they know where I live, maybe it was them.'

'Where would I find the Beaufort house?'

'They have a place over at St Mawes – they're a sailing family, own lots of boats. The house is called Lane End.'

'Thank you, Mr Villiers – I'll leave you to get some rest.'

Alexander Jameson wheeled his bicycle into the back garden and leaned it against the wall of the coal shed. Whistling, as always, he pushed open the door to the scullery, pulled off his boots and filled the kettle with water. The house was quiet but Gladys always went to help her sister on a Thursday – that was a bad do, Alexander thought to himself; Violet's husband losing both his legs down the docks – and they never compensated him, saying it was his fault – he had been careless. The kettle whistled and Alexander poured the boiling water into the tin bowl which was standing in the sink. He removed his braces and let them fall by his sides, took off his shirt, picked up the bar of soap from the draining board and began to wash. As he finished drying himself, the scullery door was opened and a little face appeared.

'Oooh, Sandy – I'm ever so sorry …I didn't know you'd be here – well, you know.'

The woman blushed scarlet and turned her head away. Alexander laughed.

'It's all right Vi – I was just 'aving a wash, come in.'

The face reappeared as soon as the naked torso had been covered with a shirt.

'What you doing 'ere anyway? Where's Gladys?'

'Oh – well, I don't know, that's what I came to ask you – I've left Gordon with a neighbour while I came over to see if

Glad was all right. I got a bit worried – she never misses a Thursday.'

'She seemed a bit peaky this morning, I thought – before I went to work. I took 'er up a cup of tea and she said she was all right – just felt a bit washed out. I don't think she's been good for a couple of days.'

As the pair talked, Alexander led the way through the kitchen and into the front room. Suddenly he rushed across to the window where Gladys was laying on the floor between two chairs.

'Gladys, Gladys – what's happened?'

Alexander saw his wife's eyes open slightly as he said her name. He bent down next to her. She spoke very quietly.

'Gladys, what did you say? Say it again, dearest.'

Glady's mouth made as if to say 'M' but no sound came. Her husband held her closer.

'Please say it, Gladys. I'm here. I'm listening.'

'Mermaid.'

'Mermaid? Did you say mermaid, my love?'

No reply came this time.

Violet knelt on the floor next to her sister and lifted her wrist. She looked up at Alexander, tears filling her eyes.

'She's gone, Sandy, Glad's gone.'

'She can't be.'

Alexander lifted his wife into his arms and stroked her hair. He looked up at Violet.

'She's not gone – I just saw her breathe – look, she's breathing.'

Violet put her hand on her brother-in-law's shoulder.

'Sandy, let her go – let her go. I'll fetch the doctor.'

Violet ran out through the front door, leaving Alexander with his wife.

Superintendent Bolton gathered everyone at the station together at nine o'clock.

'Gentlemen, we need to talk about what's going on and to update. I know you are all of different ranks and you all know and hear and see different things. Well, what I am about to say does not go out of this station. Please listen to what I've just said and understand what I mean. People in the town are starting to surmise and gossip – you know that's what the general public do best – well, I don't want to be their victim. So, if this station is leaking like a basket then there will be disciplinary action and severe consequences. In plain English, keep your cards close to your chest. Understood?'

Everyone nodded and said 'understood.'

'Gentlemen, the reason I have called you together, apart from reiterating the need for utter discretion, is to tell you that we are very much on the back foot at the moment. Constable Boase is doing a sterling job, against all the odds, but I think we need to pool our resources and do better. What I would like to do now is to collate with you the information we have so far on this investigation. We seem to be encountering new problems every day and we need to get on top of them – before there are any further catastrophes. Now, I know my predecessor Greet would never have done anything like this or been so open with you all. But, I'm different and I hope you can see a difference in the way I work. I believe that a problem shared is a problem halved and so I am appealing to you to add anything about our present work that you may know. Keep your eyes and ears open at all times – every day, every hour, every minute of every day. This is not an unrealistic expectation – it is what you are paid to do. Anyway, without further ado, let me share with you what we know, just to put you in the picture…and in no particular order or chronology.'

Superintendent Bolton took a sip of water from a glass on the desk, put on some reading spectacles and looked at his notes.

'Firstly, we have the main feature of the poisonings. What we know is that, correct me if I'm wrong, Boase, three establishments have all positively shown as having foodstuffs containing thallium on their premises. Our victims, dead or alive, ingested thallium to varying degrees. We have narrowed this down, in all probability to a commercial traveller, seemingly new to the game, who sold the products to those establishments. We need to find him. Is that correct, Boase?'

Boase, who was standing at the back of room replied.

'Yes, Sir, that's absolutely correct.'

'The next situation we have is in respect of the abortion which has killed Mrs Medlin. We have been given a sketch of the possible perpetrator, drawn by a lady called…umm – let me see, oh, yes, Alice Hole. Look at this, pass it round and keep a look out for this woman. I have it on good authority that if Alice Hole has drawn this, you may as well be looking at a photograph. Have a good look and keep that image in your mind. May I remind you, that we have two deaths due to this poisoning – I do not want any more. We have one death from an illegal activity – I do not want any more of those either. So please, please gentlemen, keep a close eye on everything. Listen to anything and everything and report back to either myself or Boase if you think you may know of anything helpful to our cases. Thank you, gentlemen and good morning.'

Doctor Stephen Pengelly closed his black bag, pulled on his coat and hat and opened the door of the surgery he was now going to be sharing with three other doctors. He had only arrived yesterday on the late train, had very little sleep and could eat no breakfast due to nerves. He thought to himself how proud his parents would be if there were still here, how proud to have a doctor in the family. He thought back to his father's words, spoken to him regularly as a child.

'Listen, boy Stephen, you can do anything in life – anything you want to and don't let anyone stand in your way. Mind to be kind though, always kind. But, one thing…don't end up like your father, no education, a lowly tin miner with bad lungs. And find a lovely woman to make your wife – and don't let her end up like your poor mother, dead at thirty-two. Always work hard to provide for her and love her as much as you can. Remember, my boy, my son – you can do anything.'

Doctor Pengelly thought that his father would never have expected him to become a doctor, but, he was, he had done it and he was going to make his parents proud – and, if possible, find a lovely woman to make his wife. The young doctor took a deep breath and went out into the street. Barely had he walked twenty yards than a middle aged woman came running up to him.

'Oh, please, Sir – are you one of the doctors? You look like you are – please, God, you're a doctor?'

Dr Pengelly looked down at the small woman, surprised to be impeded in this way when he hadn't even got to his first house call.

'Yes. I'm Doctor Pengelly. Please be calm. What is the matter?'

'It's me sister – Gladys. Oh! She's dead. Please come.'

The doctor placed his hand on the woman's shoulder.

'Please, calm yourself – what is your name?'

'Violet – me name is Violet. Please come, it's not far.'

The woman and the doctor took the short walk from Woodlane to Swanpool Street and to the house where the Jamesons lived. As the pair entered, Alexander was still on the floor cradling his wife. Doctor Pengelly went across to them.

'Please, Sir, let me…'

The doctor looked for signs of life and confirmed to the devastated man what Violet had already told him.

'I'm so sorry, Mr…'

'Sandy…my name is Sandy.'

'Well, Sandy, I want you to let Violet look after you for a bit while I take care of your wife. Is there anything you can tell me? Had she been unwell?'

'I said to Violet that she looked a bit unwell – but she said she was all right. What happened to her, Doctor?'

'Well, I don't know right now, but that's what I'm going to find out. Violet, please make some tea for Sandy.'

Boase looked at the notes that he had made during Superintendent Bolton's previous update. Three days had passed since the meeting telling everyone they had to be more vigilant. That was all very well but there weren't many clues so far. Boase leaned across the desk in the lobby and took up a pencil to make some amendments. At that moment the desk sergeant appeared from upstairs carrying two mugs of tea.

'Thought you might be glad of a cuppa.'

Oh, yes – very glad, thank you.'

'While you're here, this message came in about ten minutes ago.'

The sergeant handed Boase a note which he pulled from its envelope and read.

'Oh, no. I don't believe this. Is the Superintendent in yet?'

'Yes, I just saw him upstairs making tea. Everything all right?'

'No, not at all.'

Boase left the tea on the desk and ran upstairs to the small room that served as a kitchen.

'Sir, good morning.'

Superintendent Bolton turned, a cup in one hand and a biscuit in the other.

'What's all this, Boase? Steady on, you'll have a heart attack – and that's the last thing we both need at the moment.'

'Sorry, Sir. Look this note came addressed to me – I think it's probably more for your benefit.'

'Let's see.'

Boase handed the paper over and the older man put on his reading spectacles and looked at it.'

'Well, I'll be...'

'What do we do, Sir? Is this the same woman?'

'I have no idea but this is not good, Boase, not good at all. Do you know this family – Jameson?'

'No, don't think so, Sir. Do you want me to go and meet with the doctor as suggested – or would you rather?'

'Err...come with me. Yes, we'll go together if you can spare the time?'

Boase felt he really had no spare time but he didn't want to give a bad account of himself now – not when Irene might be depending on him; he had to do everything to get her back now and to be able to take care of her.

'Fine, Sir. Yes, I'll come.'

'Best go now I suppose – get a coat on.'

The note had come from Doctor Richards and he had asked that someone in authority came to see him as a matter of urgency. Superintendent Bolton with Boase went into the Doctor's surgery which was situated in a large house on Woodlane. A small woman wearing an apron and with several dusters tucked into her belt, came across the large hallway towards them.

'Can I help you gentlemen?'

Bolton cleared his throat.

Yes, we're from the police station, we are here to see Doctor Richards – he is expecting us.'

'Wait a moment please.'

The small woman disappeared and returned a few minutes later.

'Doctor Richards will see you now. Come through please.'

The two men followed behind and were led into a small room with a desk and a narrow couch in one corner. A tall, thin man stood up from behind the desk.

'Good morning, gentlemen. Thank you for calling so promptly.'

'I was dismayed to read your note. Boase and I have been hoping that this wouldn't happen again. Two women in fairly quick succession. What can you tell us about it all, Doctor?'

'I examined the women myself post mortem yesterday, naturally we have sent away for a full and thorough examination and reports to determine the exact cause of death – but of course, we already know this.'

'Do we? Can you be sure that this was the case for both women – your note said that they died due to an attempted abortion?'

'Yes. There was no attempted about it – both procedures were successful, unfortunately, heavy-handedness, lack of medical knowledge and no care for hygiene and cleanliness meant that both women lost their lives. I contacted you because I felt that you should be investigating this.'

Boase looked indignant.

'Doctor, we are investigating it. This second assault has only come to our attention this morning.'

'Well, I don't like to see this happening. I used to work in London – saw it all too often with awful consequences.'

'Boase is correct – we are doing our best and we do have a lead. Can I ask you, Doctor, would you be able to say if this is the work of the same person?'

'Yes, in my experience, I would say conducted by the same hand – and I would say definitely a woman. Please let me know how your investigations are going in this respect? I'm sorry, I have a patient now.'

'Yes, thank you, Doctor. Good day.'

Bolton and Boase left the surgery and returned to the station.

Chapter Nine

Boase again struggled to find sleep. He had so much on his mind. The weather had come in and rain was drizzling down his bedroom window. The night was a cold one and Boase shivered. He sat up in bed, awoken from a nightmare. A horrible nightmare. Despite the cold, Boase was sweating. He reached for a light and felt better for not being in the dark. He didn't like the way the nightmare had made him feel and this one wasn't about the war, about the trenches – no! This was closer to home - too close to home. He had had a dream of Irene – that she couldn't come to terms with her blindness and had thrown herself down Jacob's Ladder, that awful flight of one hundred and eleven steps, that vast stone staircase. She landed at the bottom just as Boase walked by – she had fallen right in front of him. He had bent down and scooped up her broken body in his arms. It was just too awful to contemplate. As he sat up in bed and thought about something like that happening, a tear fell onto his cheek. He wiped it away, angry with himself. Had he not suffered dreadful horrors in France just a few short years ago? So, why couldn't he deal with this? It was his job to look after Irene, to bring her home – to have a home to bring her to. Yes, he would prove himself to her – it was a man's place to provide for his woman, to take care of her.

Boase went down to the kitchen for a glass of water. He returned to his bedroom and pulled on some warm clothes. Back in the rear hall, he put on some stout boots and went out into the night. He always thought better when he was walking by the sea. Down the length of Melvill Road and around the back of the Falmouth Hotel, where some late revellers were strolling home in high spirits. Onward towards Pendennis Castle, taking in the sea air and enjoying the chill of the night clearing his head. As Boase walked along underneath Hunter's Path he heard someone in the undergrowth. He stopped and listened. The sound was coming closer. Boase wondered who could be out at this time of night in the cold air. He listened again when suddenly he heard a joyful bark and a very familiar canine came running out of the bushes and almost jumped into his arms.

'Topper, my old friend – what on earth…?'

The dog was presently followed by his master, George Bartlett.

'Good evening, Sir? What are you doing up here at this hour?'

'Boase? I might be asking you the very same…'

'Oh, I couldn't sleep – got the weight of the world on my shoulders at the moment. Just needed to clear my head.'

'Same here. Want to talk about it?'

The two men sat on a nearby bench. Topper continually sniffed at Boase's overcoat.

'Topper, what are you doing, leave Boase alone.'

'Umm…he may be after this.'

Boase pulled out a half-eaten cheese sandwich from his coat pocket and, breaking it into two pieces, handed them to Topper, who took them gently and then settled down, paws crossed.

'I hope that wasn't gone off, Boase. I don't want my companion to be poisoned with your leftovers.'

'That's poor taste, Sir, under the circumstances.'

Boase was chuckling now.

Anyhow, I only put it in there this morning. It's perfectly fine.'

'Good. Pleased to hear it. Now, what's troubling you?'

Boase explained to Bartlett what had been going on recently – all about the other abortion, his worry about the poisoner striking again – and his fears for Irene. The two men left the bench and walked along the sea front until it was almost light.

'Well, Boase – you'd better cut along if you've got work to go to this morning. And – I wouldn't neglect a visit to that Beaufort place over at St Mawes – there might be more to that than meets the eye.'

'Right oh, Sir. Cheerio.'

The two men went their separate ways. Boase resolved to go to Lane End today – if Bartlett thought there was something to be gained then that was good enough for him.

Boase sat in the motor car yawning. Constable Penhaligon who was driving, grinned.

'Didn't you get any sleep last night?'

'Not much. And I'm starving – got any food, Penhaligon?'

'No – sorry.'

The car turned down into a long driveway where at the end stood a rather large country house, a small mansion, Boase thought. Penhaligon gave a low whistle.

'Would you look at this – I haven't seen anything like this since that time we went out to Penvale Manor – do you remember that?'

'Yes, Penhaligon, yes I do remember – but I don't think even Penvale Manor was as grand as this. Apparently, they have their own beach. Come on – let's see what's happening.'

Boase and Penhaligon got out of the car and walked up to the front door. Boase pulled a lever in the wall and a bell rang on the other side of the door. A young woman greeted them and Boase introduced himself and Penhaligon.

'We'd like to speak with the Brigadier please, Miss.'

'Wait here please. I'll see if he's in.'

The woman returned almost immediately and led Boase and Penhaligon into the library where Brigadier Beaufort was sitting behind a large oak desk. He looked up as they entered the room.

'Good morning, gentlemen. I confess, I'm perplexed as to why the police would want to see me?'

'I'm sorry to trouble you, Brigadier – but in the light of your recent sad event, I just wanted to ask you a couple of questions. You must know we are investigating several other cases of poisoning?'

'Yes – of course I do, but I don't see what I can do to help. Just wish you'd catch the blasted fellow that did this. My wife hasn't spoken since the funeral, she's devastated I can tell you – we all are, my sons and myself included.'

'What makes you think a man did this, Brigadier?'

'What...what's that? Oh, well, I don't think that – it's just an expression, isn't it?'

'I wanted to ask you about the relationship between Edgar Villiers and your family.'

'Damn that man! He's a cad and a swine.'

'Why would you say that?'

'He has persisted in pursuing my daughter, day in and day out. I tried to warn him off but no, would he listen? No, he would not.'

'Why did you try to keep them apart – we heard she was quite happy to be with him?'

'That's as maybe, Constable – but he's nearly twice her age and a married man to boot! That's why I tried to keep them apart. But my daughter was always very strong willed – the more I tried, the more she continued.'

'What happened at the funeral between Villiers and your sons, Brigadier?'

'I'm not absolutely sure – we were all in a state of extreme high anxiety, as you can imagine. I think they went out to have a word with him but he had disappeared. So, nothing happened as far as I know.'

'Did you know that Villiers was attacked in his home?'

'No – why would I know that?'

'This happened last Thursday at about eleven-thirty, when he arrived home – can you tell me where your sons were at that time?'

'No, my wife and I retire at ten o'clock, always have. I don't know where they were – they're grown men. You'd have to ask them.'

'Are they here at the moment?'

'Yes, they're preparing to take one of the boats up to Fowey this afternoon – you'll find them down at the beach. Just take the little lane from the side of the garden. It descends quite steeply so proceed with caution.'

Boase and Penhaligon negotiated the slippery path that led from the garden down to the water's edge. Three men in sailing gear were making ready to launch a vessel. Boase called out to them and all three men turned.

'Good afternoon, I'm Constable Boase, this is Constable Penhaligon – your father said we would find you here.'

'Good afternoon, I'm Davy Beaufort, this is my brother, Carberry and here's Johnson. I'm afraid we can't chat long – tide and all that, we're off to Fowey. How can we help?'

'Well, we wanted to ask what's the situation between the three of you and Edgar Villiers?'

'Oh, him.'

Davy looked at the ground as he wiped his hands on piece of rag.

'Well, we don't like him – he's been seducing our sister when he has a wife no more than a couple of miles away in a mental institution.'

'Have you been anywhere near his house in the past seven days?'

'No, no – none of us. I'm not even sure where he lives. I know Topsy visited there often but no, we've never been.'

'Villiers was attacked the other night – by more than one man. We heard there had been an earlier upset between you at your sister's funeral.'

'Well, not really an upset. Nothing happened and, no, we certainly didn't attack Villiers. The man is a blasted nuisance but I just hope he'll give us a wide berth from now on. We have nothing now that he wants.'

'Right, thank you, Sir, I'll let you get on your way. Enjoy your day.'

Boase and Penhaligon returned to their car and went back to Falmouth.'

'Mr Villiers, please. Go home – you've had a nasty bang on the head. I'm not even sure you should be out of the hospital.'

Porky Hancock had run his butchery business in the village of Mawnan Smith, as George Bartlett always used to say, 'since Queen Victoria was in short trousers.' That always made Boase laugh. He missed Bartlett's London sense of humour.

'Mr Villiers, you are upsetting my customers, now please leave my shop.'

'But I need to tell them it was me. I'm the poisoner. It's me!'

'Yes, well, it's hardly likely that anyone is going to believe that you are a poisoner now, is it? Come along, off you go, that's the ticket. I've got joints to sort out before the rush –

and my own joints have had me in purgatory all night, I don't mind telling you. Good bye, Mr Villiers – mind how you go.'

Edgar Villiers stumbled from the shop and into his motor car. Full speed he went through the village, down the hill to Maenporth and onwards to Falmouth. He pulled up outside the police station and went inside. The desk sergeant looked up as Villiers entered the lobby.

'Good afternoon, Sir. What can I do for you today?'

'I've got a confession to make. I need to see someone. NOW!'

'Just hang on a minute, Sir. Confession? Tell me what it is you want to confess?'

'I'm the poisoner – it's me you're looking for.'

Just as Villiers spoke the words, Superintendent Bolton came down the stairs.

'I'll deal with this, Sergeant, thank you.'

'Good morning, Sir – would you like to step into my office? Sergeant, send Boase in please.'

Bolton and Boase sat opposite Edgar Villiers, notebooks in hand.

'So, what's all this about, Mr Villiers?'

'I poisoned all of those people – and now, I can't live with myself.'

'So, tell me why you would want to do that?'

'Because I hated all of them.'

'Who? Who did you hate, Mr Villiers?'

'That awful man who owns the Mermaid – the foreigner who bought George's; had a run in with him on more than one occasion…and the other one at the Rose Tearooms, I can't stand him either.'

'But…none of those people are dead. It's the customers who have suffered.'

'But their silly little businesses have suffered though, haven't they.'

Boase listened and continued to make notes. Superintendent Bolton rose from his seat.

'Mr Villiers, you are clearly not a well man. You've been badly assaulted, you're not yourself and to make a confession like this – well...really you ought to go home and get some rest. Would you like someone to see you home?'

'No – but you'll be sorry you didn't listen. I tell you - you'll be sorry.'

'Mr Villiers, be kind enough to sign in the desk diary as you leave – it's just policy.'

Superintendent Bolton saw Edgar Villiers to the front desk.

'Sergeant, give me your desk diary please.'

The sergeant looked puzzled.

'The blue book under your desk, Sergeant.'

'Oh – right you are, Sir.'

The blue diary was presented and Villiers signed his name and wrote his address in it.

'Thank you, Mr Villiers. Good day to you.'

Bolton returned to his office.

'What do you make of that, Boase?'

'I don't really know – you didn't believe him?'

'No – I think he's not well, of a good family, he couldn't really give us a sound motive – and the girl he loved so much was a victim. It's not possibly true. Also – look at this. This handwriting in the dairy...that doesn't look like the writing on the note you showed me that George Bartlett received. That note looked like a woman's hand to me. We need to find the real culprit.'

'Very good, Sir.'

Boase felt uneasy. He was of the opinion that the handwriting *did* look similar. But, he wouldn't argue with the chief.

Caroline Bartlett stood in front of the mirror and fiddled with her hair.

'Princess, you look beautiful – just like when you were a girl.'

'George, dear, stop being ridiculous. Oh...now look, the pin at the back has fallen out. Oh, I'm all fingers and thumbs today. I know she can't see us, George – but I still want to look nice when I see her.'

'I know you do, Princess. Here, can I help you with that?'

Caroline handed her husband the hairpin and he gently pushed it amongst her soft curls.

'Will that do?'

'Yes, thank you, dear. Now, hand me my hat and we really must be off – I don't want to be late, she's expecting us. Be a good boy, Topper. Look after the house while we're out.'

Topper lay on his rug and watched his master and mistress leave through the front door. He settled down again, paws crossed, and sighed.

Caroline rushed into the hospital and towards Irene's room.

'Oh, do look, George, they've pulled her bed over to the window so she can get some sunlight.'

'Irene, darling – it's Mum and Dad come to see you.'

Irene was sitting up, her hair had been brushed and a rose pink colour had come to her cheeks for the first time.

'Hello, Mum, hello, Dad.'

Her parents each kissed her and took a chair to her bedside.

'How are you, Irene?'

Bartlett held his daughter's hand as he spoke.

'All right, Dad. You know, it's strange, but they wheeled my bed over here by the window – it's so lovely and warm but it somehow seems - brighter.'

The Bartletts looked at each other across the bed, daring not to hope that there may be a small improvement.

'Well, the sunlight always makes everyone feel better. Have you had breakfast?'

'Yes, the nurse brought me some scrambled egg on toast. Tasted like rubber but I was starving so I ate it and didn't complain.'

'Well, that's good if you've got your appetite back, dear. You have lost a little weight since you've been here.'

George Bartlett chuckled.

'Wait till you're home again – your mother won't waste any time fattening you up.'

'Oh – no. I don't want to get fat. Archie always laughs when he sees fat women. No, I don't want to be fat.'

'Archie's been to see you he said?'

'Yes…I'm afraid I wasn't very nice to him – he caught me at a low ebb and I was feeling sorry for myself. I haven't seen him since. I wish he'd come back.'

Caroline laid a bag of sweets next to Irene's hand.

'Well, maybe he's finding it a little difficult, dear. You know how he feels about you.'

'Yes, Mum. Yes, I do. And I've been beastly to him over the last few months. I don't know how to put it right.'

'Well, you will. You pair of lovebirds were made for each other. It'll come right. Here you are, dear – I've brought you some sweets.'

'There you are, Irene – your mother's fat campaign has begun in earnest and you're not even home yet.'

'Stop it, George, it's just a little treat.'

'Thanks, Mum. I'll have one now.'

Boase had received a note from the Bartletts inviting him round for supper on the following Thursday. He arrived at the house, greeted by Topper in the usual manner.

'Hello, Archie. Thank you for coming.'

'Don't thank me, Mrs Bartlett – sorry, Caroline. You always make me welcome and feed me – it's me who should be thanking.'

'Don't be silly – you're always welcome here, Archie – you always will be.'

Boase and the Bartletts ate a rather large supper of chicken, boiled potatoes, carrots and cabbage. Dessert was one of Archie's favourites – treacle tart and custard. Afterwards, several bottles of Leonard's London Beer appeared on the sideboard in the parlour.

'Go on, you two...go through. I know you've got lots to talk about. George, dear – you've left your matches on the hall table.'

'Thank you, Princess.'

'Can I help with the dishes, Caroline?'

'Absolutely not, I did most of them as I went along – it's just a few plates. Go and sit down.'

Thank you – the food was lovely.'

Bartlett and Boase sat by the fire and opened their beers.

'Cheers, my boy – here's to a successful outcome on your case.'

'It's not the same without you, Sir. One minute things seem to be ticking along quite nicely, the next, I don't know what I'm doing. Take yesterday, for instance.'

'Why, what happened yesterday?'

Bartlett lit his pipe and listened as Boase recounted the story of Edgar Villiers and his visit to the station and the confession.

'The thing is, Sir, I thought the handwriting looked similar to the note you received.'

'Well, my boy, I usually trust your good judgment – but you sure you're not wanting it to be the same? Bolton is probably right – there doesn't seem much of a motive.'

'So – why confess? Why give yourself a death sentence for no good reason?'

'As you get older, Boase, you'll realise that people do strange things – things that sometimes there's no accounting for. Think about the man Villiers. He's just lost a woman he loved very much. By all accounts, his other woman, his wife, if I can make so bold as to say that, is in a mental institution. Maybe he's had enough. Sometimes, you need life experience and age to understand these things – but you, well, you saw how it was in France – the utter hopelessness, despair. Sometimes, a man can be very easily broken. I think, in the absence of any more, you have to be guided by your superior on this. Always remember, you don't earn enough to take all the responsibility – he's in charge and he's paid to take the brunt of any errors. Just you remember that. Anyway, from what I can see, you're doing an excellent job.'

'Well. I've learned everything from you, that's for sure.'

Chapter Ten

'Mum – the pain is really bad.'

Jeanette Nosworthy clutched the stone hot water bottle to her stomach and curled up tighter in the armchair.

'Come on, you'll 'ave worse than that before you die. Sit still and take these aspirin. 'ere you are, drink the water.'

Mrs Nosworthy handed the tablets to her daughter with the glass of water. She stood behind the chair and rubbed the girl's shoulders.

'You'll be all right in a minute – a woman's toils are always hard. Men don't understand. No, they don't understand – but mind you choose a good one, on who'll make you 'appy.'

'I don't want a man. I hate men.'

Mrs Nosworthy smiled.

'Well, you say that now, but – give it a year or two…'

Jeanette rearranged her cushion and closed her eyes. She hoped sleep would make everything better.

A small group of people assembled in the churchyard at St Gluvias in Penryn the day Gladys Jameson was laid to rest. Boase had heard about the service and, having just made a visit to a possible witness in Penryn, drove up the steep hill and parked on the bend in the road just outside the church gates. He entered the church midway through 'The Lord is my

Shepherd' and found a seat near the back. Sandy Jameson sat at the front with Violet and two more of Gladys's sisters. He wept into a handkerchief. As the small coffin was carried from the church, the mourners followed behind to a burial plot under a group of trees in a corner of the quiet churchyard. Boase waited near the church wall and observed the assembled mourners. He momentarily found himself wondering if there could be any link between these happenings and the poisonings. Shaking himself out of his thoughts, he realised how foolish this was – no, there was no relationship between these events.

Sandy Jameson, accompanied by Violet was the first to leave the grave. The pair paused next to Boase and Jameson regarded him.

'Aren't you that policeman?'

'Yes, Constable Boase, Sir. I'm very sorry for your troubles.'

'Well, I just wish you could find who has done this – I understand that my wife is not the only victim?'

'I'm very sorry, Sir – we're doing our best. I realise it's indelicate today of all days but, well, can you tell me anything?'

'Don't apologise – it's all right. No, I can't really tell you anything…except…'

'…except what Mr Jameson? What is it?'

'Well nothing, really. Just that, the last thing Glad said to me when she lay on the floor was 'Mermaid.'

'Oh, Sandy – that's silly; everyone knows Glad loved mermaids, had done ever since she was a little girl.'

'Yes, I know that – but why would she say that to me – just then, just before she died?'

'I'm sorry again, Mr Jameson, please accept my condolences.'

'Thank you, Constable. You're welcome to join us at the house for the wake.'

'Thank you – but no, I have to return to work. Good bye.'

Boase left St Gluvias and returned to Falmouth.

Several uneventful days passed and those days quickly became two weeks. Superintendent Bolton was becoming frustrated and Archie Boase was losing all hope of settling his cases. It didn't help that the people of Falmouth were becoming restless – local eateries were largely boycotted and everyone sensed an uncommon air of suspicion. Even food purchased from the shops was scrutinised, sniffed, dabbed gingerly onto the end of many a nervous tongue before consumption. Children cried that they didn't want fish paste on their bread anymore and the men in the docks covertly plundered more food from abroad – that would be okay…that would be safe to eat.

'Boase – would you go out to Helford today if you get time?'

Superintendent Bolton had stuck his head around around Boase's door.

'Just want to see how Villiers is – I don't think he's our man and I won't change my mind on that but Humphrey Pearce mentioned to me yesterday that he heard strange goings on in the cottage next to his in the village a couple of nights ago – nothing further reported but wouldn't hurt to keep an eye out.'

'Right, Sir, will do.'

Boase sighed and bit into an overly large slice of cake baked for him by Mrs Curgenven. Surely he had enough to do what with the poisonings and the abortionist; to be fair, he thought, Bolton had taken the latter on himself – but no one was actually achieving anything and the police were beginning to look bad. But then, if Bolton felt Villiers was innocent, why didn't he just drop it? The man had seemingly recovered from his previous ordeal and no other similar assaults or robberies had been reported.

Boase finished his cake and went out into the lobby to arrange a car to go to Helford. As he waited at the desk for some keys, a woman rushed in through the door.
'Can I help you, Madam?''
'Yes, I'm Alice Hole – I did the drawing for you.'
'Oh, I see. Well, how can I help you?'
'That woman in the drawing…'
'…what about her?'
'I've just seen her again, well, yesterday.'
'Where? Where did you see her, Mrs Hole?'
'Please – call me Alice.'
'Where did you see her, Alice?'
'Up Killigrew – she was just coming out of one of the houses there yesterday morning. It was very early – barely light…but I swear it was her.'
'But why didn't you come straight away and tell us?'
'I'm sorry, I couldn't – my Elsie was took bad in the early hours and I was running for a doctor. Nearly ran straight into her as she came out of the house – she was as close to me as you are now.'
'Right – what number was it? Can you remember?'
'Yes – number forty-one.'
'Thank you, Alice – let's hope we can find out something.'

Forgetting all about Helford and Edgar Villiers, Boase ran out into the street and over to nearby Killigrew Street about one minute away. He knocked on the door of number forty-one. No reply came. He knocked again and presently footsteps were heard on the other side of the door. A small child opened the door.

'Hello, young lady – is your Mummy or Daddy in?'
The child shook her head.
'Is anyone else in with you?'
Again, a shake of the head.
'Are they coming back soon?
'The girl nodded and slammed the door shut.

Boase was irritated – imagine leaving a child of that age alone in the house. He walked back across the road to the station and, forgetting about collecting a car for the trip out to Helford, settled back down behind his desk. He picked up the *Falmouth Packet* and flicked through the first few pages. Page four showed a photograph of the Mermaid and its owner, Leslie Pentecost, together with a story about the still unsolved poisoning cases – questioning 'were the police up to the job?' Boase cast his mind back to the funeral and his conversation with Sandy Jameson. *Mermaid.* He told Boase that his wife's last word was Mermaid. Boase leapt up from his seat! What if...he hadn't even thought until now – what if the abortions had something to do with the Mermaid? What if the abortions were connected to the poisonings? Boase looked out of his window and onto the street. He tried to collect his thoughts. No. That couldn't be – how could these events all be tied in together? But, yet – why not? He needed George Bartlett's help now. He just had a feeling – something wasn't right here but he couldn't put his finger on it. He decided to visit Bartlett that very evening – he would know what to do, Boase was sure of it.

And so it was that at half past six that very same evening, Boase was knocking on the door at Penmere Hill, hoping that the Bartletts wouldn't be too busy. He hated to turn up unannounced or uninvited but this was vitally important now. Caroline Bartlett opened the door and looked surprised.

'Oh, Archie – I'd forgotten…was it tonight we'd invited you? Oh, my dear, I'm so sorry – I really thought it was Friday. George - Archie's here.'

'No – it's fine. You haven't made a mistake – I'm just calling on the off-chance of seeing Inspector Bartlett.'

Caroline laughed loudly. Boase thought how much her laugh sounded like Irene's.

'Inspector Bartlett – Archie, you do make me laugh. You can call him George, you know.'

'Well, thank you, I know – it just feels a bit, well, umm – awkward.'

'Come on in – don't stand on the step. Come on.'

As Boase entered the hallway, Topper, who had been standing behind Caroline, came forward and licked Boase's hand.

'Hello, Topper boy. You're very quiet – thought I'd come to the wrong house for a minute there. Didn't get my usual welcome.'

'He hasn't been himself, Archie – George thinks he's missing Irene. He's a bit off his food too.'

'That's no good, Topper – got to keep your strength up for when Irene comes home. She won't like to think you're not well.'

'Archie, my boy, good to see you. What brings you here?'

Bartlett came out of the parlour, pipe in hand.

'I'm so sorry, Sir. I wouldn't have bothered you but I really need to speak to you.'

'That's all right, Boase. Caroline – room for one more at the table…?'

'…of course, dear.

'Oh, no – I couldn't. That's very kind of you though. But I really couldn't.'

Bartlett pulled Boase's sleeve and led him into the parlour.

'Boase – I'm sure you could. I heard it might be apple crumble – and I know you like a nice bit of apple crumble with custard?'

'Well, George, I've laid the place now so he'll have to stay.'

'Thank you both very much.'

'Well, it's almost ready I think, Princess? That just gives me enough time to pour you a beer, my boy.'

Bartlett and Boase sat enjoying a beer and waited for the food to appear. Boase felt a little uneasy – it didn't really seem right to be here without Irene. But this evening he was on business so that was a little different. The trio sat at the table and tucked into a beef casserole. Topper sat next to Boase's chair.

'I'm worried about Topper…never seen him so quiet. I hope he's not unwell.'

Boase had pushed three pieces of beef to the side of his plate and, when he had finished, he offered one of the pieces to Topper. The dog sniffed the meat in Boase's hand and turned away.

'Please, Topper – it's lovely best beef. Try a bit. Go on – for me.'

Boase offered the meat again and Topper licked it this time. Gently he took the meat from Boase's hand and placed it on the floor.

'Go on – eat it, it's very nice.'

Topper picked up the piece of meat and, carrying it carefully, placed it on Irene's empty chair.

'Oh, George – he's saving it for Irene.'

Caroline's eyes filled with tears.

'Don't worry, Princess, I'll work something out for the old man – don't worry, Topper, I won't let you be so upset. Now come on – you eat this bit of meat yourself.'

Bartlett took a second piece of meat from Boase's plate and handed it to Topper. This time, he ate it.

'Oh, George, dear – it's as if he knows and understands what you've said.'

'Of course he understands, Princess. Don't worry, old boy. I'll sort it out for you. Now come with Boase and me – we've got business to discuss and we'd like your company.'

'Can I help you clear away, Mrs Bartlett?'

'No, not at all, Archie – I won't hear of it, but thank you all the same.'

Bartlett and Boase poured another London beer and talked about what had happened in the recent investigations.

'I really need your advice, Sir. What do I do next?'

'Well, my boy, I think I would be trying to find out if there is a link between the poisonings and the abortions – stranger things have happened. Did Mrs Jameson have some connection with the Mermaid, the boat, and was that what she was trying to tell her husband?'

'I don't know – you don't suppose Leslie Pentecost is the abortionist, do you, Sir?'

'I don't think so – it's usually a woman, although not confined to the fairer sex. Why would he be doing that? What credentials could he have that would enable him to do it?'

'Well, we know that, whoever it is, isn't very good – look at the mayhem they've caused.'

'True. Drink your beer.'

Boase drank his beer and Bartlett puffed on his pipe.

'Maybe I would visit Pentecost and try to find out if he knew this woman – what the relationship was, if any. You might turn up something there?'

'Maybe worth a go – thank you, Sir. Yes, I'll try that. It might be a start, which is more than I have at the moment.'

'Good man – now, will you have another?'

'I don't think so, thanks, I've had two already.'

'That's nothing – go on…it'll help you to sleep. Then I won't have to bump into you in the middle of the night out at Castle Drive.'

'As I remember, you bumped into me because you couldn't sleep either!'

Bartlett chuckled.

'You have an answer for everything – that's what I like about you, in a funny sort of way…and you've got a good brain. You'll figure this one out, I know it.'

'Well, it's good to know that you're in my corner. I know I shouldn't be asking you…'

'Well, no one is going to know, are they? I won't tell anyone.'

Thank you, Sir, I really appreciate your help. Truly I do.'

Boase stayed until half past ten. Caroline had gone to bed and the anticipated soporific effects of the beer were beginning to become a reality. Bartlett and Boase yawned in unison.

'Right, Sir – I should get off. Thanks for everything, and thank Mrs Bartlett for the delicious food. Top notch, as always.'

'You're always welcome here, Boase, you know that. Now, don't forget to keep me posted on events, and let me know if I can help. See you next time. Mind how you go.'

'Good night, Sir – and thank you.'

Boase tripped over the step and stumbled to the garden gate.

Bartlett smiled and locked the front door. Topper had settled into bed and Bartlett was ready to do the same.

Boase had a headache. He went downstairs to the kitchen where Mrs Curgenven, anticipating his late return the night before may warrant some good food to start his day, had left him a bacon sandwich. Boase ate it, washed down with two mugs of tea and began to feel better. A brisk walk into work and he began to return to normal. He now had a plan. He was going to pay a visit to Leslie Pentecost – maybe Bartlett was right; this may be the start he needed.

At ten o'clock, Boase took the short walk to the Prince of Wales pier and enquired amongst the few boatmen if they had seen Pentecost. He was pointed in the direction of a small café nearby and he went there to find the object of his search sitting at a window seat drinking tea and eating a bun. Boase walked across to the man.
'Good morning, Mr Pentecost – could we speak, please?'
Leslie Pentecost looked up.
'Oh, it's you – again. What am I supposed to have done now?'
'Well, that depends. Possibly nothing but I need to talk to you.'
Boase sat in the seat opposite and looked at Leslie Pentecost. As he stared at him, he really couldn't imagine him being capable of what he was thinking about. But, he was here now, and he had no better idea.
'Mr Pentecost – do you know the name Jameson? Gladys Jameson?'
'No. Should I?'
'No – but please think. Have you ever seen that lady? Do you recognise her name?'
No – I never 'eard of 'er.'
'Are you absolutely sure?'
'Wait a flippin' minute…Gladys Jameson…'
'Yes…do you know her?'
'That's the woman that was found dead 'ere a couple of weeks ago. That's 'ow I remember 'er name. You're kidding

me… you don't think I 'ad anything to do with that lot, do you?'

'I'm not saying that, Mr Pentecost, I'm just trying to get information about what happened to her.'

'Well, try somewhere else. I didn't even know the woman.'

'All right – but, do you think you had any mutual acquaintances?'

'I wouldn't know – why?'

'Do you perhaps remember her dining on your boat – on the Mermaid?'

'I 'ave no idea. I don't always see all the people that come aboard – quite often I'm not even there – that's what I pay my staff for. So, no – I can't 'elp you.'

Boase, disappointed, thanked Mr Pentecost and left the café.

Archie Boase fiddled with a pencil. He walked across to the window. Just why had Mrs Jameson said '*Mermaid*'? Maybe he had read too much into the whole thing – maybe she had lapsed into near-unconsciousness and it was all just nonsense. And yet…no, he couldn't get that out of his mind; there must be something. As he opened up a new bundle of notes to catch up on, Constable Penhaligon knocked on the door and entered.

'Sorry to interrupt you – but Superintendent Bolton asked me to give you this note…he's just had to rush out.'

Penhaligon handed the note to Boase and left the room. Boase read the contents and sighed. Bolton was reminding him that he had failed to go to Helford and now, apparently, there had been another incident in the village. Boase got up and went out into the lobby, grabbing his coat and hat from the stand as he left. As he drove through Mawnan Smith, a small crowd was gathering outside Porky Hancock's butcher's shop. Boase stopped the car, got out and walked across the road to the shop. He pushed past the group of onlookers and saw

Porky sitting on a chair at the back of the shop. Boase dispersed the people and closed the shop.

'What's happened, Mr Hancock – you okay?'

'Well, one minute I was in the shop serving customers, the next I heard breaking glass out the back…I ran into the sitting room and two men were in there going through the cupboards. I shouted out and one of them came right up to me and hit me with something. I fell on the floor and two of my customers came and picked me up and set me down on this chair.'

'Did you recognise the men?'

'No – they had their heads covered, with black balaclavas. No, I couldn't see their faces.'

Boase pulled up another chair and sat down next to the butcher. He pulled out his notebook and a pencil.

'Can I get you anything? Cup of tea?'

'No, oh – a glass of water perhaps. Thank you.'

Boase went through the door back into the house and filled a glass with water from the kitchen tap. As he was returning, he looked down at the floor and saw a kind of pin, like that from a lapel badge. He bent down and picked it up. As he stood, he looked again – there was the associated badge. He picked that up too and returned to the shop. He handed the man the glass of water.

'Do you want me to take you to the hospital? Are you quite well? You've had a bit of a knock. Mind if I take a look?'

Boase examined the back of Porky Hancock's head.

'Well, there's no blood – but you'll have a bit of an egg there tomorrow.'

'And I'm sure I can find a nice bit of bacon to go with that, Constable.'

The two men laughed.

'Well, go careful – if you feel unwell, I want you to see a doctor. Now, look at this – do you recognise it?'

Boase held up the lapel badge.

'I'm sorry, I can't find my glasses – what does it say on it?'

'It's got a flower on it – mean anything to you?'

'Wait – my glasses are here in my pocket. Show me again.'

Boase handed over the badge.

'Yes – that's a magnolia. They hand these out for exclusive members of the Magnolia Club. They tried to get me to join once – I wasn't interested. I think if you're one of these members to get a vote on the board and suchlike. Yes, that's definitely the Magnolia Club.'

'And so, I take it it's not yours?'

'Absolutely not. Do you think one of the men in here dropped it, Constable?'

'Well, unless you've had company…'

'No. I live alone and no one comes here. The only people I ever see are my customers – and they only come into the shop.'

'Can I take this badge with me?'

'Be my guest, please do.'

'Now, remember what I said – if you feel unwell…'

'Yes, I know. I've got to reopen the shop anyway. I've got people waiting.'

'Well, you know best. Don't overdo it.'

Boase continued on to Helford and, after finding nothing of note, returned to Falmouth. He went straight to the Magnolia Club. As he expected, the place was closed. These types of clubs never opened until late in the evening and stayed open until the early hours. The police could do nothing but as long as there was no trouble, the constabulary appeared happy to turn a blind eye. Crossing to the small sweet shop opposite, Boase resolved to return to the club later that evening. He left the shop with a large bar of chocolate in his pocket and went back to the station.

Chapter Eleven

Irene Bartlett sat up in bed and brushed her hair. She smoothed the sheet and blanket and waited for her parents to arrive. Minutes later George and Caroline appeared. They each pulled up a chair next to the hospital bed.

'Hello, Irene my lovely – you're looking a bit better today. You've got some colour back in your cheeks.'

'Thanks, Dad. I feel a bit better. The doctor has been to see me this morning. He said that if I continue to improve, I could come home in a couple of weeks.'

Caroline grabbed her daughter's hand.

'Irene dear – that's such lovely news. Oh, I can't wait to see you back in your own room – I've got so much to do first.'

'Mum – you haven't got to do anything. You're not well. Anyway, the doctor says that I have to learn to manage my disability – to get used to it. That's exactly what I intend to do. Besides, it may get better – there's still a small chance my sight may be restored.'

'Well, please God, that happens for you.'

'You all right, Dad? Have you heard from Archie?'

'I'm all right, Irene. Archie was with us for supper – wanted to ask me a few suggestions about his work. It was nice to see him. Has he not been in?'

'Not for a while.'

Caroline patted her daughter's hand.

'Well, we know he's very busy – he told us his boss is expecting a lot, didn't he, dear?'

'Yes – he seems to have his work cut out down there. He asked for you when he came to us.'

'It's okay, Dad.'

'Oh, I almost forgot – your mother's been shopping. Look at all this stuff she's bought…oh, Irene – I'm sorry.'

'Dad, please, it's all right. It's just a turn of phrase. It's fine. What have you brought me then?'

'Well, you know what's she's like. Let me see – chocolate, sweets, a bar of lavender soap, a new comb and brush set and some pocket handkerchiefs.'

Thanks, Mum, that's really kind of you. Can you put them in this little cupboard, please, Dad?'

George Bartlett obliged and the three sat and chatted about nothing in particular for the next half hour until it was time to go. George and Caroline kissed their daughter goodbye and took the short walk back to the house. They talked as they walked along.

'George, dear – why do you think Archie hasn't been in to the hospital?'

'Well, he has, Princess – just not lately. He told us how busy he is. I think you're reading too much into it.'

'Do you think he still loves her?'

'I know he does. It's not going to be easy if they get together – they'll both have to get used to things if she doesn't improve.'

'If they love each other, they will. Look what we've come through – love has got us through it all.'

'Don't start that kind of silly talk now, Topper will hear you. Come on – in you go.'

Superintendent Bolton chewed on the end of an already-chewed pencil. Next he drew a sketch of a mad-looking feline with two staring, blazing eyes. He regarded the sketch, rolled up the piece of paper into a ball and batted it into the wastepaper bin. He sighed audibly. He stared at his desk thinking what he should do – he didn't want higher authorities up the line intervening and interfering if this present business didn't come together...but what to do? His thoughts were interrupted by a sharp rap on the door. The desk sergeant appeared with a mug of tea.

'Thank you, Sergeant. Everything okay?'

'No, Sir. I'm afraid not. We've just had word from the hospital that a young girl has been admitted – looks like she tried to rid herself of her unborn baby – or they suspect that someone assisted her.'

'What? Oh, dear God – not again. I'd better get on up there.'

Bolton pulled on his coat and his hat and rushed up to the hospital. As he entered the main corridor he could hear a woman screaming. He saw a doctor and two nurses running into a side room; minutes later, the noise had stopped. Bolton went to the main desk where a young nurse was making some notes.

'Excuse me, Nurse – my name is Superintendent Bolton from the Falmouth Police Station - could I see the doctor who is in charge at the moment please?'

'Would you wait here please, Sir? I'll fetch someone.'

The nurse returned a few moments later with the doctor.

'Superintendent Bolton – I'm Doctor Carter. How can I help you?'

'Can we speak privately, Doctor – please, if you wouldn't mind?'

'Of course – here, we can go into this room, if you wish.'

The two men sat in a small, cramped side room which looked like it had previously been used as some sort of store.

'Doctor – what can you tell me about the girl that was brought in – having tried to end her pregnancy? You must talk to me because I'm investigating more than one incident of this recently – as you may know. I have to find out who is doing this…I can't allow it to continue.'

'Well, Superintendent – I'll help you as much as I can. No one likes to deal with this sort of business – never mind the law, as a doctor, I find it downright intolerable. The girl is just sixteen years old – her name is Jeanette Nosworthy. I can't allow you to talk to her today – she's in a lot of pain at the moment…we've just given her some treatment, including sedation so you'll have to leave it for now.'

'And the baby?'

'The baby is no more, I'm afraid to say. Terrible business – hope you can hurry up and put a stop to it all. Anyway, I must get on – let me know if I can help any further and maybe look in again tomorrow after lunch?'

'Thank you for your help, Doctor - I appreciate it. Goodbye.'

Doris Pellow stared at the man sitting at the table opposite her own in the Pyramid Café in the centre of Redruth. She had just been to visit her father at the Meadowbank Home, meeting her mother on the omnibus at Lanner. Doris's brother had been killed in 1918, a few days before the end of the Great War. Unable to cope with the news, her father had gone into a decline until eventually, having a mental breakdown, he had been admitted to the home for the insane. Doris's mother went each week with her daughter to visit and when they left they came to the Pyramid Café for a cup of tea and a cake or sandwich. The man opposite caught Doris's gaze and turned his head towards the window.

'It's good your father is seeming better, Doris, love.'

Yes – I do believe he is, Mum. Did you hear what the doctor said? That if he continues to progress, he might be right as rain and back home in a couple of months.'

'I know, dear – that's marvellous news. I can't wait to have him back where he belongs – it's been such a long time.'

Doris leaned across the table towards her mother and lowered her voice.

'Mum, see that man over there? Don't look now – look in a minute...do we know him from somewhere?'

A moment or two passed and Mrs Pellow looked across at the man. Possibly feeling her stare, he turned from the window and looked straight at her. She looked away.

'Yes – I grant you, he does look familiar. Can't say as we know him though. Maybe he works in somewhere we've been?'

'Don't know, Mum. It's starting to get right on my tripe now – you know when you just can't place someone?'

'Well, stop thinking about it and maybe it'll come to you.'

The two women left the café and waited at the bus stop by the railway station for their return transport – Mrs Pellow to Lanner and Doris to Falmouth. As they waited, Doris revisited the conversation.

'Mum – that man...I think he knows me.'

'Whatever do you mean, Doris?'

'Well, I saw him looking at me a couple of times – as if he knew me.'

'Well, you were looking at him as if you knew him – don't be silly now. Just forget it.'

The rain came down all evening and late into the night. Doris Pellow awoke with a start. She sat up in her bed in the small flat she shared with Iris Harcourt. The flat was over a shop in Market Street and looked out over the harbour. Sweat dripped from her brow and her heart was racing. She lit the room and got out of bed. Kenneth the large ginger cat who shared the accommodation most nights and ate his evening meal there, although the two women suspected he had a daytime home too, stretched at the end of the bed, looking indignant at being woken up at two o'clock in the morning.

'It's all right, Kenneth – just a bad dream. Go back to sleep.'

Kenneth yawned, stretched out one paw and curling back into a ball, promptly fell asleep.

Doris went across the hall and into the small scullery She turned on the single tap and cupped her hands under the flow of water. Feeling better and cooler for splashing the icy water onto her face, she poured some into a glass and took it back to her bedroom. Kenneth was asleep and Doris climbed awkwardly into the bed, trying not to disturb her feline companion. Lying down, she couldn't get comfortable and the nightmare that had awoken her now revisited her more vividly than when it had jolted her from her sleep. It was the man from the café in Redruth – *that was what her dream was about*! That strange man who she had stared at – and who had stared back at her. She lay in the darkness now, comforted by the sound of Kenneth's tiny snores and feeling his breathing on her foot. There was no chance of sleep now – she couldn't stop thinking about him; but not in a good way. No, she had a bad feeling about him but not something she could put her finger on. Her mother had always said she was a good judge of character and now – now she felt uneasy and, strangely, nervous.

Superintendent Bolton walked to the Falmouth Hospital to see if he could speak with Jeanette Nosworthy. He was allowed in to see her with her mother but for no more than five minutes on account of her still feeling so unwell. As he entered the small ward, Jeanette's mother rose from her seat.

'It's all right, Mrs Nosworthy, please sit.'

Jeanette lay in the bed looking for all the world like a little ghost, so pale was her skin.

'I'm sorry to trouble you, Jeanette – and you, Mrs Nosworthy, but I am obliged to investigate what happened. I need you to be honest with me.'

Mrs Nosworthy looked at the Superintendent anxiously.

'Sir – will we go to prison, Sir?'

'No – you won't go to prison but you absolutely must help me – do you think you can?'

'Well, we'll try – won't we, Jeanette.?'

'Yes, Mum.'

'You won't make her tired will you? The doctor says she's lost an awful lot of blood.'

'No – I won't keep you long. Do you know who did this to you, Jeanette? I don't need to know why you did it, I do understand more than you think – but I most stop this happening to anyone else – you're very lucky to be alive, I have to say.'

'My husband threatened to kick her out on the street – he's very handy with his fists, Sir. We didn't know what else to do – so I tried to make arrangements. The woman said it would be all right.'

'Do you know this woman?'

'No – she came to us one night and said she had heard we needed some help, you know. All she said was her name was Rose. I didn't ask no more questions, me and Jeanette just wanted it dealt with and to get back to normal.'

At this point, Mrs Nosworthy began to cry. She held Jeanette's hand in her own.

'Jeanette, I'm so sorry – I should have stood up to that brute. I'm so sorry – please forgive me. I've been such a fool...and that man I married, well, he's got a short memory. You don't know this and I possibly shouldn't say but, well, what with everything that's gone on. Me and your father – we had to get married. I was already carrying Jane and my parents made us get married – and yet, there's one rule for him and another for his daughter. He's disgusting!'

'It's okay, Mum. Please don't cry.'

'Ladies, I need to ask you – before I go…is this the woman who came to you?'

Bolton showed Alice Hole's picture to the pair.

'Yes! Look Jeanette, that's her. Yes, that's Rose. I'm sorry – that's the only name she gave.'

'Thank you, both – you've been extremely helpful. I may need to come and see you again – or send another policeman…that okay?'

'Yes – and thank you, Sir. Thank you so much.'

Boase had no luck revisiting the Magnolia Club – he had interviewed the owner, Bertie Fairbrother, but the best he could offer was a list of the VIP members. Boase felt it made for some interesting reading but little more. He would never be able to establish who had dropped the badge – and then it might not even be the real owner. He would have to employ some other method to deal with this.

Cynthia Biscoe opened the shutters in the Rose Tearooms. The early morning light filtered through into the restaurant. Cynthia had been the manageress at the tearooms for four years. She looked at her wristwatch – it was almost ten past nine. Doris wasn't usually late for her shift. She looked out of the window and saw the girl hurrying up the hill. She rushed through the front door.

'Mrs Biscoe – I'm so sorry…'

'It's all right, dear – I was just getting worried, you're usually so punctual.'

'Yes – I had such a terrible night and then I overslept. It won't happen again.'

'Don't panic dear, just help me open up, will you?'

As Doris went round laying up the tables, she suddenly stopped in her tracks. *That was it!*

The man in the restaurant in Redruth – and in her nightmare. He was the man visiting the poor mad woman in the asylum. The man who turned up in the really fast motor car. That was it. He had brought the woman, must be his wife, Doris had thought, down into the visitor's sitting room where Doris had sat with her mother and father the week before. That's probably why he was staring at her – he thought he recognised her too. Doris continued with her duties – but she was still not satisfied. She knew she was right and yet, she had seen that same man somewhere else – but where? She continued with her work, puzzling over the strange man for the rest of the day.

At eight o'clock that evening, Esme Shepherd arrived at George's Café and, opening her ledger, proceeded to empty the cash from the till. She knew everyone would have left. She muttered to herself.

'This till is short again. Look sixpence again – and sixpence on Thursday. What on earth is happening? Well, if this continues…this is the last time.'

'Boase – step into my office, would you? I have some news.'

Superintendent Bolton held open the door and Boase went into the room.

'They've caught the men – the robbers from Mawnan Smith, well, I say robbers, they weren't any good, all they managed to do, it turns out, was to steal a total of about five pounds and assault two men.'

'How were they caught, Sir?'

'Apparently that new, young village bobby caught them red-handed; trying to take money out of the post office cash register...but they couldn't open it. They'd even tied up the postmistress but she broke her bonds and ran out into the street right in front of the policeman. He whistled and help came. They've admitted to other offences. What a useless bunch! Anyway, they won't be doing that again.'

'That's very good news, Sir – very good indeed. What about the Magnolia Club pin? I couldn't get anywhere with that?'

'I don't know – threw you off the scent, didn't it? Probably something else they pinched. Anyway, one less thing to worry about...we're beginning to lose credibility and I don't like it. At least it looks like some progress has been made – even though we weren't directly responsible for it. Do you have any further news on anything?'

'No, Sir – I'm sorry, enot a thing to report yet.'

'Well, don't despair – we'll get a break soon.'

'Yes, Sir, I hope so. Thank you, Sir.'

'George, dear – what time are you collecting Irene from the hospital?'

'It's still two o'clock – you've asked me about ten times! I've told you – the doctor has to see her and sign her out then she can leave.'

'I'm sorry, George, I'm just worried I won't get everything done in time. Do you think she'll be hungry when she arrives?'

'Princess – she's coming from half a mile up the road, not half way round the world. I'm sure she won't be hungry but if she is, she'll let you know.'

'Don't get snappy, dear – I was only asking. Now, I've made a lovely cake for her, and some sausage rolls – oh, and those little buns she likes, just in case she wants a snack. Now, what about her tea this evening?'

'I'm going out to the shed. I'll leave you to finish preparing for the siege. Coming Topper, boy?'

Topper, who had been hanging around the kitchen for the duration of the cooking marathon, followed his master and, looking back longingly for one more morsel, went out into the garden.

'Irene, I have to say that you've done so well – you've come such a long way in the last couple of weeks. I want you to keep up your excellent efforts and your positivity. I can see there's some, albeit small, improvement in your sight – and I know you can only see shadows and maybe a few vague outlines, but, that's better than you were. I can't promise you anything more – but keep on as you are and never give up hope. And remember lots of fresh air, rest, sleep and good food. Irene – I wish you all the very best, you're such a lovely young woman. Make sure you come back when your check-ups are due, don't miss any.'

'Thank you so much, Doctor Bailey – you've been very kind, and all the nurses have been lovely to me. I appreciate everything you've all done. Now, my father will be here in a minute – I don't want to keep him waiting.'

'No, make sure you're ready. Come with me and I'll sit you in the lobby – the sun's just come around to that side, it's lovely and warm. Here, give me your arm.

Irene and Doctor Bailey walked slowly out to the lobby and Irene sat down to wait for her father.

Chapter Twelve

Boase had taken a rare afternoon off work, in fact, it had been Superintendent Bolton's suggestion; he felt that Boase was looking tired and maybe not quite being as productive as usual – he could see he was feeling the strain and he didn't want him to become unwell, indeed, such an asset he felt the younger man to be, losing him now to sickness would be a catastrophe. And now Boase, glad of the opportunity, walked along Market Street for the third time looking in the shop windows. Bartlett had told him that Irene was coming home and he really wanted to buy a welcome home gift for his girl. Well, if she still was his girl. Boase was unsure on this one – but he wanted to get her back. He continued to look at all the beautiful things she would have loved before – but now, well, now she couldn't even see them. Should he just buy something lovely anyway? And risk upsetting her?

Boase continued to browse for another half an hour and reached the Parish church. He looked up at the clock; it was nearly half past two. He turned and looked again at the jewellers across the street. He went over and into the shop. A young girl came out from behind the counter.

'Good afternoon, Sir. How may I help you?'

'Umm…well, I'm not really sure. I'm looking for…well, umm…'

The girl smiled sympathetically.

'Is it for your lady? You want to buy a gift for her?'

'Yes, Miss. That's right – but, it's a little difficult.'

'All ladies are difficult to buy for – so I'm told, but we have some lovely things here. How much did you want to spend?'

'No – I'm sorry, you don't understand. My lady – she's blind. And I don't want to upset her because she can't see what I've bought for her.'

'Oh, my dear – I'm so sorry. Well, don't despair, I'm sure she'll love whatever you choose.'

'Yes, I hope so. Miss, do you have any ideas – could you help me?'

'I think I can – I've just had a brainwave. How about a pomander?'

Boase looked at the girl, blankly.

'A what?'

'A pomander – look, I'll show you. This is possibly the best idea I've had in ages.'

The girl smiled at Boase as she unlocked a small mahogany and glass cabinet.

'Here – this is a silver pomander, look you fill it with scent and you can hang it around your neck as a pendant. So, that way, she can smell your gift – even if she can't see it.'

Boase held the silver pomander and looked at it. He didn't speak.

'I'm sorry – is that a bad idea?'

'Oh – no, it's such a lovely idea, so thoughtful, thank you. Is it very expensive?'

'It's two pounds and ten shillings.'

'Oh. I'm sorry – I don't have enough for that.'

'Well, we do terms if you were interested?'

'How much would the deposit be, Miss, and how long until I can have the item?'

'Well, could you put down ten shillings? We charge a modest rate and you can take the item today if you wish? You need to give us your details and make arrangements to pay weekly or monthly.'

'So – I could have it today? Really – that would be excellent. Thank you, yes, ten shillings – here you are, Miss, thank you so much.'

'You need to decide what you would like to put in it – the traveller gave us some samples to show how to use it...I can give you one of those if you like, no extra charge. You can choose, let me see, I've got rose, lily-of-the-valley, lilac...'

'You have lilac? Please may I have that?'

Boase's voice cracked as he thought of Irene and how her beautiful hair always smelled of lilacs. He couldn't wait to see her again. He made the purchase, had it gift wrapped and thanked the jeweller's assistant profusely

'They're here, Topper, they're here!'

Caroline Bartlett heard the taxi pull up outside the house and ran to the door, almost tripping over Topper in the process. She opened the door and ran into the front garden, opening the gate as Bartlett helped his daughter from the taxi.

'Irene – oh, my dear girl, it's so lovely to have you back where you belong. Let me have your bag. Topper, Topper, get down.'

Topper, overjoyed to see Irene after such a long time, could not contain himself at her return.

'Leave him, Princess – you can see how excited he is.

'Yes, dear, but I don't want him to hurt Irene.'

'He's fine Mum. We'll have a big cuddle when we get inside, Topper – I've been looking forward to it.'

Boase, correctly thinking that Irene would be tired and probably wanting an early night, sent a note to the Bartlett's asking if he might visit Irene tomorrow evening – and that if the small boy he had sent with the message didn't return to him, then he would come to the house at six o'clock if that would be all right. No note came by return and so, Boase employed his time preparing his clothes for the visit. He looked several times at the gift he had purchased, still worrying if it would be okay.

Edgar Villiers sat in a large armchair at the Meadowbank Home for the Insane. His wife sat in another, looking out of the window across the gardens. She turned to her husband. He rose from his chair and went across to her.

'Eunice, are you all right – can I get you something?'

His wife looked at him and shook her head. He looked at her face and saw the woman he had married, how beautiful she had been, those lovely big eyes are what he fell in love with all those years ago; now they were empty, muddy pools – and it was all his fault.

'Well, it's going to be your bedtime in a minute or two, dear, so I'd better be off. Look, my dear, I'm not sure when I'm going to be back again – but I'll try not to leave it too long. I have some business dealings to contend with urgently, but I'll see you again before long. Now good night, God bless, pleasant dreams.'

Edgar Villiers kissed his wife's forehead and went downstairs to inform the Matron that he was leaving.

Falmouth quickly became enshrouded in a strange sea mist that evening. Boase looked out of the back door, in a welcome break from starching his clothes in preparation for his visit to Irene. It was dark now and becoming chilly. Bartlett stood on the back step at Penmere smoking his pipe. Topper stood next to him. It was about nine o'clock and Caroline and Irene had gone to bed, both exhausted. Topper yawned and returned to the house and got into his own little bed at the foot of the stairs.

Doris Pellow finished her evening shift at the Rose Tearooms and was making her way down High Street. She had promised to come back with fish and chips for herself and Iris and was now heading to Renowden's at the bottom of Killigrew Street to get them. As she approached the shop, people were still queuing outside. Nobby Renowden made the best fish and chips anywhere. Doris joined the queue and began chatting to a girl she knew from school, Peggy May. The two girls talked until it was their turn and, taking their food away, went their separate ways. Doris had forgotten her gloves and the warm paper felt nice on her hands. She didn't know what happened next. Her assailant pulled her into Bell's Court behind Market Street and only a few yards from her home. The fish and chips fell to the floor and Doris was lifted off her feet. She could tell this was a man – but nothing more. He was behind her, his strong hand across her mouth. He spoke in a low voice.

'I've seen you watching me – staring at me. Well, I recognised you too. Now – if I should see you again when I'm visiting my wife, don't even look at me, do you understand? And you don't tell anyone of this little meeting either – because they'll never believe you over me. More importantly, if you should remember where else you've seen me, you may already remember…but if you try to tell anyone, you will be in deep trouble, I give you my word. Understand?'

Unable to speak, Doris nodded. She kept her eyes closed and then collapsed, falling to the ground.

It was at twenty minutes past midnight when a night watchman saw something on the ground in the beam from his lamp. He lifted his lamp higher, spreading the beam. He hurried over and found Doris, not moving. He lifted the girl up – she was cold to the touch.

'Help, help – anyone about? Help. *Help I say!*'

A sash window above the court opened and a man leaned out.

'What's all that racket – people trying to sleep up 'ere.'

'Sorry – there's a woman here – not sure if she's dead.'

''ang on – I'm coming.'

The man from the window appeared in combinations, trousers with braces by his sides and unlaced boots. He had brought another light.

'What's 'appened to 'er?'

'I don't know – I was just checking the doors up in the court and then I saw her in the shadows. Is there a doctor or someone who can help?'

'Wait – there's a nurse lives above me…I'll see if she can come.'

The man ran back up the court and into his building. He returned presently with a young woman in dressing gown and slippers and with rags in her hair.

'This is Phyll – she works at the hospital. What do you think, Phyll?'

The young nurse tried to examine the woman as best she could in the darkness.

'Well, she's not dead – I think she's frozen. We need to get her inside.'

The man from the window volunteered.

'Bring her into mine – my wife will make her a hot drink.'

'Yes, that's what she needs for a start – and a drop of brandy?'

Both men now laughed

'I ain't got no brandy – will a drop o' rum do instead?'

'I'm sure she won't complain.'

The two men carefully carried Doris, who had now begun to stir, into the house where they laid her on a couch by the fireplace, with some dying embers still glowing in the grate. She was given hot tea and rum and presently, her colour returned and she was able to sit up.

'What happened to me?'

Phyllis pushed a cushion behind Doris's back.

'It looks like you might have been attacked. We need to tell the police.'

'Oh…no, please don't, I'm okay – really I am.'

'You probably banged your head when you fell – I'm a nurse, please trust me. You need to get looked at properly in the morning and, yes, the police need to know.'

'I don't remember anything – there's nothing to tell them.'

Phyll, when she was sure that Doris was well enough, allowed the two men to take her home, with the recommendation to wake up Iris on her return and ask her to keep an eye on her for the rest of the night – and for her not to return to work for a few days. Doris complied – but with no mention to Iris of what she had remembered happening.

'Are you looking forward to seeing Archie tonight, dear?'

Caroline drew back the curtains in Irene's bedroom and straightened the bedclothes.

'Yes, Mum, very much. Will you help me to find something nice to wear? I don't want to look shabby.'

'You could never look shabby, Irene – you're beautiful. What about that blue dress that Archie always liked you in?'

'Yes, yes, I'll wear that.'

'I thought your father and I would leave you alone in the parlour, you must have so much to talk about in private – I'll put out some cold food for you.'

'Thanks, Mum – although I'm sure I don't know what we'll talk about.'

'You'll soon find plenty. He still loves you, Irene.'

'Why would he love a blind woman?'

'Because he sees deeper than that – because he loves you. Do you still love him?'

'More than my life – but I'm not going to tell him that because I don't want to ruin his.'

'Irene – tell him. He was distraught over what happened between you before. You must tell him – if you still want him. Now, there's a cup of tea right next to you on the table – can you manage?'

'Yes, Mum, thank you.'

'And look – Topper has come to see you. Turns out he came upstairs last night and slept outside your door. Probably wanted to make sure you were all right.'

'Well, I am – so stop fussing and start taking care of yourself please, Mum.'

Caroline left the bedroom and Topper came round to Irene's side of the bed and rested his chin on the counterpane.

Irene felt for the cup and saucer.

'Oh – that's why you wanted to come in, is it? Mum's brought me two ginger biscuits. Go on then – one for you, one for me.'

Archie Boase got out of bed early. He examined his clothes again and looked at the gift he had bought for Irene. He went downstairs. Mrs Curgenven had left a plate in the bottom oven of the range. Boase looked inside and withdrew the plate. There were sausages, bacon, mushrooms and fried bread with two eggs. Boase placed the breakfast on the table. He fetched a knife and fork and sat down. He felt a little strange in his stomach. He pushed the plate away. He felt nervous about what might happen this evening. What would he do if she didn't want to be his girl anymore? Well, he had to find out tonight. He couldn't stop thinking about her, that was for sure but, if she didn't want him, well, he'd have to deal with that blow.

Boase took a biscuit from the pantry on the way out through the scullery door and ate it, walking through the garden. As he walked along Western Terrace, a woman came running out of a garden gate and ran straight into him.

'Oh…young man, I'm so sorry, oh dear, my cat was just chased by a very big dog and I'm afraid she may have been bitten. The dog ran off and the cat ran out here. I was worried she had run into the road. I don't know what to do.'

The woman looked very upset.

'Well, maybe the cat has run back into the house?'

'Do you think so? I'd better look. Oh, whatever shall I do?'

Despite the sense that there was much overacting going on her, Boase felt rather sorry for the woman.

'Let me have a look too – I'm very early for work anyway.'

'Young man, you are a saint. A saint, I say. Come with me.'

Boase followed the woman back into the garden and into a long hallway. She went to the end of the hall and into the kitchen.

'She often comes in her because the range is always warm. It doesn't look like she's here now. Oh dear, whatever shall I do?'

At that moment, there was a scratching sound back out in the hall. Boase and the woman returned there and listened.

'I think she's closer than you think, Madam. Shhhh.'

They listened again. Boase knelt on the floor.

'She's under here.'

'Well how on earth can that be? Are you sure?'

'Yes, listen again.'

They waited and this time, more scratching followed by a tiny whimper.

'Have you ever had these boards up?'

'No – I've only lived here just under a year. There were several people renting before I came so I don't know what they did.'

Boase followed the line of the skirting board and, pulling a large chest of drawers away from the wall, found a hole in the floorboard – just big enough for a cat to squeeze through he thought.

'I've never moved that chest of drawers, young man – it was here when I came, think the owner probably didn't want it.'

Boase was on his hands and knees and with his strong arms and hands, pulled up one floorboard.'

'Sorry – but if she's coming out, this will have to come up.'

'Oh, please do not apologise – you're so very kind. Do what you need but please get her back.'

Boase pushed his arm through the newly made gap and felt warm fur under his hand. He grabbed suddenly and pulled out one very pathetic looking tabby cat. He handed her to the woman.

'Oh, my dear soul – what can I say? How can I ever repay you? A thousand thank you's.'

Boase felt like he was watching some awful theatre performance and felt sure the woman must have previously been on the stage.

'I'll try to make it good but I'll have to be quick. I need to get into work.'

'Well, please don't worry – no one will see it when the chest is pushed back.'

'This is a lovely big house – do you live here alone?'

'Well, almost – there's a woman living upstairs, she rents one room but I barely see her. I think she was here before but lived down on this floor. When I came she asked if she could stay on but only wanted the attic room – which suited me. I'm a widow so the bit extra money helps. Oh, talk of the devil.'

The hall door slammed shut. Boase looked up just as it closed.

'That was her. Don't know what she does all day – but it's not my business as long as she's quiet and pays her rent.'

'Well I suppose you can't ask for more than that.'

Boase strained as he tried to fit the board back in place. It didn't seem to fit so well this time. He lifted it again and peered into the darkness underneath. There was something wrapped in newspapers and rags and which had lifted up above the level of the floor. He pulled the bundle out of its resting place. The woman had gone into the kitchen to see to the cat and give her some food. Boase unwrapped the contents and was aghast. He didn't know much but he knew enough to understand what he was looking at. Looking up and down the hallway, he hastily piled everything into his haversack with his packed lunch. The floorboard now slipped effortlessly into place and Boase stood up and pushed the chest back against the wall. Having being thanked profusely by the woman, he left, she none the wiser as to his actions.

Boase knocked on Superintendent Bolton's door and entered.

'Good morning, Boase – did you have a pleasant afternoon off yesterday?'

'Yes – thank you, Sir. That was appreciated. I need to talk to you, Sir. It's urgent.'

'Oh, all right, sit down then. What is it?'

Boase relayed the events of his walk into work and the story of the cat and the woman. He then revealed the contents of his bag, showing what he had found at the house.

'That's unbelievable, Boase. No wonder it was hidden under the floor. Do you suspect the woman as our abortionist?'

'No, I don't think so – she doesn't look like Alice Hole's picture and she's only lived there less than a year – this equipment looks older than that...and look at the date on the newspaper. Although...'

'...what – although what?'

'She has a lodger living on the top floor – she was living there as a tenant before this woman arrived.'

'Could it be her then?'

'I didn't see her – but that can be remedied. This may be nothing to do with our present case, although the newspaper date is only two years back.'

'Want me to deal with it?'

'If you like, Sir, I have got rather a lot on at the moment.'

'I know...that's why I'm offering.'

I don't think there will be any point in going now – seems that the woman upstairs goes out all day, every day. Best wait till tonight probably.'

'Right, Boase – thank you. Let's hope this is the lead we've been waiting for – we're due some luck.'

Chapter Thirteen

Boase had important, no, possibly life-changing plans this evening; he didn't want to have to work, important as it was, Irene had to come first, before work, before anything. The chief was more than capable – it was his case to begin with…let him have the glory if anything came of it. Unusually, Boase clock-watched for the rest of the day. He managed to tie up lots of loose ends which satisfied him but he couldn't wait to leave. Having been home, via the strange woman's house on Western Terrace, washed and changed, Boase was now making his way to Penmere. He was trying to think of what to say, but nothing came to him and he decided to wait and see what would happen. He knocked on the Bartlett's door and fiddled with his collar. He could see Topper through the glass, bouncing up and down. Caroline came to open the door and Boase went inside.

'She's really looking forward to seeing you, Archie. You look lovely by the way.'

Boase flushed pink.

'Thank you.'

'Just be as you were and act normal – I think that's what she wants.'

'Right. Thank you.'

Boase followed Caroline into the parlour where Irene sat by the fire. Boase couldn't stop looking at her. She was perfect.

'Irene, Archie's here. Now, where's your father? We're going to the pictures. George...George, dear. It's time to leave. Now, Archie – there's lots of cold food here on the table. Both of you take what you want. There's meat, cheese, bread, pickles and some cake.'

'Thank you, Mrs Bartlett. See you later.'

Caroline patted Boase's shoulder and kissed Irene's head. Bartlett poked his head around the door to say hello and was promptly dragged out by his sleeve.

'We're already late, George – and you know I can't walk that quickly. Have a lovely evening – keep the fire in will you, Archie, please?'

'Of course. Have a lovely evening.'

'You too – 'bye.'

The front door shut and Boase and Irene were alone. They both spoke together.

'No – you first.'

'No, please, Archie – what were you going to say?'

'I was going to say that you look so beautiful and that I've missed you so much.'

'Have you Archie, dear? Come and sit by me. You must be cold. Come closer to the fire.'

Boase sat on the floor at Irene's feet and she put her hand on his shoulder.

'That's my favourite suit – the dark blue one.'

'Yes.'

'You look so handsome in that – all the girls will be chasing you.'

'No girls will be chasing me.'

Boase looked at Irene. He realised how much time they had wasted.

'Archie, you're staring at me.'

'I can't take my eyes off you. You're so beautiful.'

'Stop being silly.'

'Irene, kiss me, please.'
'Archie Boase – you're very forward!'
'I'm sorry.'
Irene giggled.
'Come here then, I'm not moving.'
Boase turned and knelt in front of her. He put his hand on her cheek and pulled her to him. He kissed her on the lips and whispered.
'Irene, be mine forever?'
'I'd like nothing more. I've been worried that you wouldn't want me anymore, the way I am.'
'You'll always be perfect to me, you must know that. I have something for you – I hope you'll like it.'
'What is it?'
Boase took the little case from his pocket and placed it into Irene's hands. She felt the case and opened the lid.
'I'm sorry – I wanted to bring you a gift to show how much you mean to me…I hope I haven't upset you?'
'Don't be silly – why would a gift upset me?'
'Because…well, never mind.'
Irene had removed the pomander and was rubbing her fingers across it.
'Oh…it's a lilac pendant. It smells of lilacs, how beautiful. Thank you. Put it on me, Archie.'
'The girl in the shop said you can refill it. I thought your favourite scent might cheer you up.'
'Thank you, dear Archie – you know how much I love lilacs. How thoughtful you are. Maybe one day…'
'…yes, one day you'll see it, I'm sure of that. I want to make you well again.'
'I'm getting better all the time – if I could just begin to see a little…'
'…you will. I know you will.'

Archie Boase held his girl in his arms and kissed her cheek. She was back where she belonged – and so was he.

Boase walked home deep in thought. He hadn't expected that Irene would want him – how he'd hoped, but this was more that he could have wished for. He reached home and went in through the scullery door. He went to the pantry and cut an exceptionally large piece of fruit cake and made some tea. That done, he retired to bed and, for the first time since he could remember, he slept like a baby.

'Sir, I'm sorry – that woman you brought in last night is demanding to see you. She says you can't keep her here; that's she's done nothing wrong.'

Superintendent Bolton looked up at the desk sergeant.

'Boase will be here in a minute – I'm not doing anything until I've spoken to him. Give her a cup of tea and some food if she wants it, will you?'

'Right o', Sir.'

Boase appeared ten minutes later and the desk sergeant indicated that Bolton would like to see him.'

'Okay – let me get my coat off, at least.'

'Be quick – think there's a problem.'

'Oh, Lord! I'm on my way. Any tea?'

The sergeant handed him a mug that was already on the desk.

'Have this one – just been poured.'

'Thank you.'

Boase sat opposite Superintendent Bolton.

'I arrested that woman last night. Daisy Poole she says her name is. She couldn't give me any answers. The time she's been living there fits in with previous reports of these…errr…procedures. She looks remarkably like Alice Hole's picture – I think she's our woman.'

'So, what now, Sir?'

'Well – we only have one person who might be able to identify her, Jeanette Nosworthy. All the other victims we know of are dead. Jeanette is our only hope.'

'Oh, I see.'

'What's on your mind, Boase? We need to put a stop a stop to this.'

'Yes, Sir. I understand that.'

'Well – I've got a lot to do today, as I'm sure you have. Can you arrange for Jeanette to come in?'

'Well, I would, Sir, but she's still recovering in hospital. She's not expected to be allowed home for another week.'

'Right. Well that woman stays put.'

Boase left the office feeling uneasy. This didn't seem right – to keep this woman here with such little evidence. It seemed all too perfect. He went back into the lobby and approached the desk sergeant.

'Has that woman in the cell had any breakfast?'

'No – I was just going to take her this.'

'I'll take it.'

Boase carried the tray to the cell and, placing it on the floor, reached into his inside pocket for Alice Hole's sketch. He looked at it carefully then replaced it into his pocket. He unlocked the cell door and entered. The woman was laying on the bench with her back to him. She turned as Boase entered.

'Good morning, I'm Constable Boase – I thought you might be glad of this.'

'I'll be glad to be out of here. I've done nothing wrong. I want to go home.'

'Well, I'm afraid that's not possible just at the moment. Here, please have this – you must be thirsty.'

The woman sat up and drank some tea. Boase was watching her.

'I'll leave you alone.'

He left the cell, locking it behind him. He took the sketch from his pocket again. He wasn't sure about this – she did *resemble* the sketch, but…

So it was at half past five, that Boase was back at the Bartlett's house. Irene hugged him tightly and everything seemed immediately better.

'This is a lovely surprise, Archie, I didn't expect to see you.'

'Well, it's lovely to see you but I do need to see your father. Is he in?'

'He's just doing something in the back garden. I'll call him.

Bartlett wiped his boots on the mat and came into the kitchen.

'Come in here, Boase while I wash my hands.'

The two men stood in the kitchen and Boase relayed his worries about the woman they were holding – and about the sketch and his worries over lack of evidence.

'Well, you may be right to be worried – but he's the boss and you have to go along with his decision. If he messes up, then that's on his head, not yours. Just go along with it – when the young woman comes in and either recognises her, or otherwise, then make a decision as to what happens next – or Bolton will. Try not to worry – I know how conscientious you are. At the moment, catching the poisoner should be your main aim, I'd say, not that I'm dismissing the other you understand, but don't neglect your duties with regard to the poisoner.'

'Thank you, Sir.'

'Now – you staying for a bit of food? You may as well now you're here?'

'Well, that's not why I came…'

Irene came into the kitchen.

'Please stay, Archie – Mum's just come back. We're just going to make some dinner.'

'You've twisted my arm. Thank you, I'll stay.'

Boase watched as Irene felt her way around with Topper beside her almost acting like her eyes.

'She's doing well, Boase. I'm so proud of her.'

Bartlett and Boase were sitting in the parlour.

'And look at that fool dog – he hasn't left her side.'

'I can see that, he's a good boy.'

'Certainly is.'

Constables Eddy and Coad ran into the lobby of the police station. They muttered something to the desk sergeant and knocked on Boase's door.

'What do you two want now?'

Boase was grinning. For the first time in ages he was feeling more settled and even happy. Irene was firmly back in his life. Eddy spoke first.

'Archie – there's been another attempt…another young woman tried to get rid of her baby last night. She's in the hospital. She's expected to pull through – but we got called up there at two this morning. The Superintendent hasn't come in yet, I know he's mainly dealing with it – but I thought you should know.'

'But – *how*? Oh, Lord. So what about the woman we have here?'

Eddy shrugged his shoulders.

'I don't know. But it can't be her, can it?'

Boase felt churned up again.

Violet Billings looked at Constable Rabone across the street. He was looking in the haberdasher's window. She watched as he checked the side door to the shop was locked. She didn't know what to do. She didn't want to cause a fuss in the police station. She crossed the street.

'Excuse me, Constable.'

'Yes, Madam?'

'Could I speak to you for a moment, please?'

'What can I do for you?'

'I just wanted to tell you…something…umm…my name is Mrs Billings. Mrs Violet Billings. It was my sister, Gladys Jameson that died a little while back.'

'Oh, yes. I know.'

'Well, something just came to me – it might be nothing but I felt I should tell you. No one could understand why my sister's last word was 'Mermaid.' I thought nothing of it – my sister always loved stories of mermaids when she was a child, well, even when she was grown up – so it didn't seem strange to me when she uttered that word. I just thought she was either in pain, or didn't know what she was saying – you know, not making sense like.'

'Go on.'

Rabone had pulled out his notebook and began writing.

'Well, I remembered something from a while back – but I can't remember who told me, or even why we were talking about it, but someone said that a woman called Esme Shepherd had bought half of the Mermaid floating restaurant. I don't know any more – I've never been on it…bit out of my price range…'

'…mine too, Mrs Billings.'

'Well, it's probably nothing – but I just wondered if my sister meant anything by it, anything about Esme Shepherd. I've probably got it all wrong as usual, but I just wanted to try to help – and I've been racking my brains ever since it happened – trying to think of anything. I'm probably just being stupid.'

'Not at all, Mrs Billings. Not at all. I'll make sure the people who need to know are told – just in case…you never know. Now just give me your address should we need to ask you anything else.'

Esme Shepherd emptied the till at the Rose Tearooms and counted the money. The restaurant was in darkness, save one small oil lamp still burning in the corner. She took the lamp in one hand and, picking up the money in the other, climbed the stairs to the office. She set down the lamp and went across to a large safe in the corner of the room. By the dim light, she could just manage to open the safe. She put the money bag inside, together with some papers and receipts. She felt in the back of safe and pulled out a small box of chocolates. She looked at the box, then, pulling down the skirt that was riding up over her rather large hips, she put the box back. Locking the safe, she crossed the room and picked up a bottle of wine from the shelf and headed back towards the stairs. She descended to the half landing then stopped. Looking at the bottle of wine, she retraced her steps and went across to the safe again. She unlocked it once more and pulled out the chocolate box. She extinguished the lamp and left the building by the side door.

'Slow down, Rabone – you'll do yourself a mischief.'
Constable Rabone came running through the front door of the police station, tripped over the mat and almost knocked Boase's tea from his hand.
'Where's the fire?'
'I'm so sorry – I've just come from the hospital. There's been another one!'
'Another what?'
Boase let Rabone get his breath back.

'A woman tried to have her baby got rid of last night. I thought the woman in the cell was the one doing all this?'

'Well, looks like we're wrong, Rabone. I'd better go and break the news to the chief.'

Superintendent Bolton listened and then, to Boase's horror, made the decision to keep Daisy Poole for another day. He had said that the events last night didn't exclude the woman; she could be an accomplice. Boase had felt a bit unnerved by this decision but could say nothing. In the end, Daisy Poole remained for another two days.

No one was really sure how Esme Shepherd was found – a message was sent to the hospital and from there forwarded to the police station. What was a fact was that Esme Shepherd was suffering from thallium poisoning.

Superintendent Bolton perched on the corner of Boase's desk.

'I need you to look at this woman's house – this Esme Shepherd. I've spoken to the doctors at the hospital; they've said she'll be okay but she's not well enough to talk to us just yet. Here's the address, take Coad and Eddy with you and search the entire place – no stone unturned.'

'I'll do my best, Sir. What about Daisy Poole?'

'Well, looks like I was mistaken – but all the clues appeared to be there. She looked like the picture, the equipment was found at her house…but I was too hasty. She says she's going to put in a complaint.'

'I'll be off then, Sir.'

'Happy hunting, Boase.'

Boase felt a bit angry – he thought that Bolton had been rather impulsive and they were not really supposed to use their cells for more than a night or two, but, well, the damage was done now. He took Coad and Eddy and went along to Esme Shepherd's house on Greenbank Terrace. The house looked rather grand Boase thought. The three policemen entered and Boase gave instructions on how best to conduct the search.

'Take away anything that looks suspicious – check under the sink and any outbuildings in the garden…look for any remnants of recent meals – look at absolutely everything, I don't care how long it takes us. The woman may have eaten out, we don't know that yet and we can't ask her but, she may also have brought something in here and eaten it. Check the fireplace, the ash bins, don't miss anything. Keep me updated – I'll start in here.'

Six hours later, the three emerged. They had several bags and boxes of items that they wanted to have analysed. Boase arranged a car to take Coad and Eddy back to the station with the items they had retrieved. The things bundled into the car, Coad turned to Boase.

'You not coming back with us?'

Boase was tired and hungry. He was thirsty too.

'No. I need to look at something else. I'll see you tomorrow. Well done – and thank you.'

Feeling exhausted, Boase sat on the wall outside the house and thought. If nothing was found amongst the things they had seized, what then? Thirst getting the better of him, he took the short stroll to the Star and Garter for a small beer. He sat in the window, there were very few people around and he was glad. He looked out across the harbour and remembered coming over to Falmouth from Redruth as a boy to take part in the regattas and rowing competitions. Such happy days before the war. Boase had grown up a lot since 1916. Now – well, now he just wanted a quiet life, with Irene. He wasn't going to let her go again, no, he wouldn't give her any reason to doubt him. He would love her as much as he could, give her everything she deserved and make her well again. He finished his drink and walked back to Esme Shepherd's house. Something wasn't quite right he felt. He went into the house and into the drawing room. A small desk in the corner had intrigued him, particularly since it was locked. Boase didn't want to cause any damage but felt he wouldn't be doing his job properly if he didn't look inside the desk. He tried the drawers again and the little cupboard at the top. No use. He looked around to see if a key had been hidden in a vase or behind a clock – all the obvious hiding places one might think of – to no avail. He searched for an implement to pick the locks but could find nothing of use. He looked through his pockets and pulled out his pen – the lovely pen that Irene had given him last Christmas. He carefully removed the gold clip and inserted it into the keyhole. He jiggled the clip around, taking care not to break it. He tried again. Something gave under the clip. He pulled and the drawer opened. Before anything else, he reassembled his pen and put it back into his pocket.

Boase pulled out three account books and lots of notepaper with scribbling and notes on. He looked at the books. He was puzzled by the titles on the covers. *Rose, George* and *Mermaid.* He almost couldn't believe what he was seeing. He leafed through the books – all showing monetary values for the eating establishments. Profit, loss, staff records – a ledger for each restaurant. So – the message he had been given about Violet Billings – about her sister, Gladys, and the Mermaid…Boase sat down in an armchair and rubbed his forehead. He wished Bartlett was here right now. What did this all mean? Something was going on but how could he figure it out? Gladys Jameson had said 'Mermaid' – her last word on this earth. Did that mean she knew that Esme Shepherd had an interest in the Mermaid? More than an interest looking at these ledgers. Was Esme Shepherd the last person to see her fit and well before Violet and Sandy had arrived? Boase had a headache. He looked again in the drawer which appeared to be some sort of 'master drawer' as he was able to push his hand down inside and release the drawer underneath. He gasped as the contents were revealed.

Boase pulled out the same type of equipment as had been found in the house on Woodlane. So did this mean that Esme Shepherd was the woman they were looking for? Superintendent Bolton had thought that about Daisy Poole then backtracked. Boase collected together what he had found in the drawer. As he closed the desk back up, he looked above his head. There on the wall was a small photograph in a silver frame. He reached up and took the photograph down. He took Alice Hole's drawing from his pocket. This was the same woman! No mistakes this time. He pushed the frame into his pocket next to the sketch and, closing up the doors, left to return to the police station.

The police station was in near-darkness when Boase returned there. The lobby was lit as usual and two policemen were on night duty and with a night watchman on patrol. Boase put his collection into his desk drawer, locked it and walked home.

Chapter Fourteen

Daisy Poole had been released. Esme Shepherd was still in the hospital and the word was that she was rather unwell. Superintendent Bolton and Archie Boase sat in silence. Boase stood up and walked to the window.

'What next, Sir?'

'Our hands are tied in a way, Boase. We can't deal with the Shepherd woman until she's well enough – who knows, she might even die. If she doesn't, then Jeanette Nosworthy has to be well enough to come in and identify her as the woman who has been going round doing these hideous acts...well, obviously Jeanette can only speak for herself. What we know is, from the evidence you gathered at the Shepherd woman's house, that she is the woman in Alice Hole's drawing and she look to be the woman conducting these...these...procedures.'

'Do you know, Boase – when I came here as a temporary stand-in, I thought to myself, this seems like a nice quiet little town and might be a welcome change from what I'm used to – how wrong I was!'

'What I can't understand, Sir, is how Esme Shepherd came to be a victim of our poisoner – I mean, she has her own victims and now she's one herself. How did that happen?'

'Well, it seems our poisoner is rather prolific. We just need to wait and see what the results from the woman's house show...if there's any thallium about.'

153

'But she may have had it out somewhere else?'

'Yes, well, there's not much we can do about that. Let's wait and see.'

Boase had made an arrangement with Irene to take her out on the Sunday. She hadn't been anywhere since she had come home from hospital and Boase wanted to treat her.

'George, dear – do you think Irene will be all right today, going out I mean? I'm so worried.'

'Princess, don't worry – Boase won't let anything happen to her. Shhh – she's coming down, she'll hear you.'

Irene stood in the hall.

'You look lovely dear. I've always liked that dress on you.'

'Have I got the buttons all done up, Mum?'

'Yes, I think so – let me have a look. Yes, you're perfect. Archie will be here in a minute.'

'Is my hair right at the back? I haven't got much left after the poison.'

'It's looking lovely, Irene – and it's actually growing back thicker than before. Are you going to keep it short do you think – or grow it long again?'

'Oh, I don't know, Mum – it needs to be easy for me.'

'Well, you can do whatever you like dear – I like it both ways. Where are you off to today?'

'I don't know – Archie says it's a surprise.'

'Talk of the devil – I'll let him in.'

Bartlett opened the front door and Topper jumped straight up from his basket and ran to greet the guest.

'Hello, Topper – how are you? Come on, let me get in.'

'Hello, Archie – thank you for taking me out. Could you please help me with my coat?'

Boase held the coat so that Irene could slip her arms into it. He leaned forward, kissed her cheek and whispered in her ear.

'You look absolutely beautiful, Irene. Come on – I've borrowed a car.'

Caroline watched as the couple crossed the garden and got into the car.

'Have a lovely day out, both.'

'Are you warm enough, Irene?'

'Yes, thank you, Archie.'

The little car wound its way round the narrow lanes until it arrived at Maenporth.

'Archie – you know this is my favourite place, I could feel we were coming here – thank you. Do you remember that day we walked here across the cliffs? That was such a beautiful day'

'We'll do that again soon – when the weather gets warmer. Are you hungry?'

'A bit – but I bet you are!'

'Well, it just so happens, I have a picnic hamper full of your favourite things.'

'Oh – how lovely you are. And what about your favourite things?'

'My favourite thing is right here next to me.'

Boase kissed Irene's hand. It made him so sad when he looked into her eyes and she couldn't see that he was doing it...but he knew she felt it.'

'Do you want to get out Irene, or eat in the car?

'I don't mind – it's a little chilly for sitting out perhaps?'

'Yes, probably – here, let me open your window – get some sea air on your face. You're looking so well, Irene, really getting your colour back.'

The young couple sat and ate their lunch. They talked and laughed. Boase helped Irene out of the car and walked her down to the water's edge. They stayed at Maenporth until it was almost dark. Neither wanted the day to end. But they both knew now that there would be plenty more like this.

A week passed uneventfully. Bolton's superior upcountry had threatened to intervene but Bolton had deflected this always unwelcome intervention from headquarters. The news came early one morning that Esme Shepherd was recovering well enough to be interviewed. Bolton and Boase went up to the hospital at eleven o'clock as planned with the doctor. They entered the hospital lobby and sat waiting on two chairs by the main entrance. A young nurse came along to speak to them. Boase was glad it wasn't Phyll – he'd made a fool of himself that time. Anyway, how could he even look at another girl – when he had Irene?

'Mrs Shepherd's doctor is just finishing her notes and he'll come and collect you in a few moments. He'll take you to her. She's up and dressed but she doesn't have permission to leave without the doctor seeing her first.'

Bolton rose from his seat.

'That's perfectly all right, Nurse. We don't mind waiting. Thank you.'

As he spoke, Boase was leafing through a woman's magazine that had been left on the chair. As he turned another page an article appeared about the latest wedding etiquette for this year. He looked at the pictures of brides and grooms and wondered. Should he propose properly to Irene? They had been engaged, yes, but then, with everything that had happened, she hadn't worn the ring again. Should he ask her again? Thoughts of weddings and wedding etiquette churning in his mind, he didn't even hear Superintendent Bolton speaking to him.

'Boase. Boase? Come on – the doctor is beckoning us.'

'Oh, I'm so sorry, Sir. I'm right here.'

'When did you take up reading women's magazines?'

Bolton was grinning as they walked along the corridor.

'Good morning, gentlemen, I'm Doctor Collins – I've been looking after Mrs Shepherd. I need to sit in with you, if you don't mind, we don't allow police interviews with our patients which are unsupervised, I'm afraid.'

'That's all right – you know what's she's accused of?'

'Yes, I had heard. We've actually just allowed, can I say, one of her victims, home yesterday? We took pains to ensure there were no encounters between the two when we heard what you say she's done. Anyway – shall we go in to see Mrs Shepherd…I'm sure you're also busy just like me?'

The three men walked into Esme Shepherd's room. It was empty. Doctor Collins looked at Bolton and Boase.

'I don't understand – she was here sitting on the bed only ten minutes ago.'

Doctor Collins ran out into the corridor.

'Nurse! Nurse!'

Three nurses appeared.

'Find Mrs Shepherd – check the lavatories and the grounds – quickly!'

The nurses departed. Bolton and Boase ran outside and into the road. Looking up and down, the main street of Killigrew was empty.

'I can't believe this, Boase. How on earth did this happen?'

'I don't know, Sir – I'll go for a car and some men – we'll find her, I'm sure.'

Boase collected a car and instructed others to do the same. Taking Penhaligon with him they drove back up Killigrew Street.

'Penhaligon – you keep a lookout on your side. Check the terraces as we go by then we'll come back and drive around those too.'

'But she could be anywhere…look at all these gardens and alleyways.'

'I know, Penhaligon. We should have had police on her door – we were given the impression that she was too unwell to go anywhere and the hospital thought it would look intimidating to the patients and their visitors. Now look where that's got us!'

Boase continued to drive, one eye on the road, one eye on the side streets and gardens. He carried on and into Penryn. This was impossible. Penhaligon turned to Boase.

'We'll never find her - she might have got on a bus. She could be anywhere. What shall we do?'

'I don't have an answer. We'll carry on a bit longer but I'm not hopeful. As the evening drew in, Boase returned to the station. The other searchers had returned already and Bolton had just arrived, having also participated in the search.

'Thank you for your efforts everyone. I'm sorry, we, so far, seem to have wasted the day. I'm going to put word out around the county, by the usual methods, to look out for this woman. My impression was that she was extremely unwell and, it seems that the hospital made a fairly last-minute decision to release her from their care. I feel totally responsible – but they only informed me this morning that she could be interviewed, not that she was actually leaving.'

Bolton returned to his office to prepare notifications and to plan a strategy to find the escapee. Three days passed and Esme Shepherd was still at large. Superintendent Bolton called Boase into his office.

'Boase, can you please show to me again the ledgers you took from Shepherd's house?'

'Yes, Sir, I'll fetch them.'

Boase returned with the books and gave them to Bolton.

'Have you been able to discover anything about her involvement with these places?'

'No, sorry, Sir. No luck. I just don't understand how she appears to be involved in establishments that have had outbreaks of poisoning and then she herself is a victim? Surely that's puts her off our suspect list – well, for this part of it?'

'Not necessarily, Boase. She could be our poisoner as well – maybe slipped up and poisoned herself? Stranger things have happened – never say never in this job.'

'Tell me what you've done to find out about her links to these places.'

'I asked the owners we already know – they've all said they have 'silent partners' – when they went into the business they were not to find out who the partner or partners were. That was a condition of a share in the business – apparently it's not uncommon.'

'Well, there must be a way of finding out – I don't know anything about business but there must be a way.'

Edgar Villiers knelt at Topsy Beaufort's grave and placed a small posy of violets there.

'Oh, my dear girl – I hope if you're listening, you can forgive me. I never thought this would turn out this way. I'm so sorry – and I miss you. I'll never forget you, my beautiful girl.'

As he turned to leave the grave, he saw Constable Penhaligon walking along the side of the fence on his way home. The two men looked at each other and walked on.

'Good morning, Penhaligon – everything all right? You're normally in before now.'

Boase leaned on the desk as Penhaligon spat on a rag and wiped it across his boots.

'I've been to the library actually.'

Boase laughed out loud.

'What for? You can't read!'

'When I was a child, I always liked chemistry and experiments. My father taught chemistry in Truro.'

'Well, blow me down. I never knew that – you never said. Did you not fancy becoming a teacher like him – instead of this lark?'

'Well, yes, but the war got in the way – and mother became ill and we just never seemed to have enough money. Shame, but there it is.'

'Yes – so what were you doing in the library?'

'Borrowing this.'

Penhaligon reached into his haversack and pulled out a large book. He flicked through the pages as Boase waited patiently.

'I had a copy of this as a boy – it's a directory of scientists and inventors. They update it each year but this one goes back a bit. Fortunately, this was the only one they had in the library – but it suits me very well. Look.'

Boase looked at the page that Penhaligon had his finger in.

'Who are they?'

'These are the credentials of winners of prizes awarded to scientists, inventors, that sort of thing. I always wanted to be in this book when I was a boy. Too late now.'

'But – why are you showing this to me?'

'Don't you recognise this picture?'

Penhaligon was pointing to a photograph of a man that he had recently recognised.

'Look – it's Edgar Villiers.'

'Villiers?! What's he doing in there?

'He was awarded the Fletcher prize for Chemistry in nineteen hundred and two. Not quite sure what he did but must have been good to get a mention in here. I think it tells us here somewhere. I'll have a proper look when I have a minute.'

'Don't bank on having many minutes today, Penhaligon. The chief has plenty of work for us all to be getting on with. Interesting about Villiers though.'

The rest of that day was spent trying to track down Esme Shepherd. Bolton's superiors upcountry had discovered what had happened and were arranging to come down within forty eight hours. Boase paid an uninvited visit to George Bartlett that evening. The two men sat in the parlour.

'If it was Irene you were wanting, she's gone out with her mother, visiting. Think Caroline is trying to get everything back to normal.'

'Yes, that's probably for the best, Sir. Anyway, it's you I really wanted to see. I'm in a bit of a fix with these cases. I could do with some guidance – if you would.'

'Well, I'm happy to help if I can – you know that. How about we open a bottle of beer and you tell me all about it. I'll need to know everything mind.'

The two men opened some Leonard's London beer and sat before the fire in two armchairs.

'I don't know where to begin really – so much has happened.'

'Well go back to the beginning – in order. Let me tell you what I know so far.'

Bartlett lit his pipe and thought for a moment.

'What I know is that you have a woman performing illegal acts on expectant mothers – and you have a poisoner. That's a start. Are they connected?'

'I don't think so – but there's something odd about all of it. Esme Shepherd appears to be the woman we're looking for in connection with the baby fiasco – but she wouldn't poison herself?'

'What if she was trying to cover her tracks – put you off the scent?'

'What do you mean?'

'Well, if I was going round poisoning people – the best way to take the heat off myself would be if I was also poisoned. If she knew what she was doing, she could just give herself a little – maybe she made a mistake. It's happened before. Not saying this is the case but don't dismiss it.'

'I'll keep it in mind. Now, Penhaligon made a strange observation today. He found Edgar Villiers in a directory of prize-winning scientists. I don't really understand what he was on about – apparently he won some prize in nineteen hundred and two.'

'Well – I don't know anything about that I'm afraid; you know what Penhaligon's like – he's a good sort though, will always help if he can.'

'I know he will. Now the Shepherd woman has gone…'

'Yes, that was rather foolish if you want my opinion – she should have been guarded…what was Bolton thinking of? Anyway, that's not my business.'

'I don't think we'll find her.'

'Well – she might slip up, if you're lucky. You've got a big job on your hands though. Bit of a lash-up really.'

'I know – we were hoping the Nosworthy girl would be able to identify her.'

'What else?'

'Nothing really – but I need to find out more about the link between Esme Shepherd and the three eateries. No one will tell me anything, well, fact is, they don't seem to know. Would you go into business, Sir, with someone you didn't know?'

'Probably not, but peoples' greed gets the better of them and they carry on regardless. Let me see what I can find out – don't worry, I'll be discreet. Don't forget, I might not be local but I know lots of people.'

'I know you do, Sir. Thank you – any help would be appreciated. I don't mind telling you, I'm stumped.

'Leave it with me, but I'm not promising anything. Another beer?'

Bartlett and Boase sat chatting until almost ten o'clock. There was no sign of Irene and Caroline when Boase left. He had hoped to see his girl, even just for a minute. He went home, deep in thought about what he had just discussed with Bartlett.

Chapter Fifteen

The day was uneventful until, at half past three, Superintendent Bolton burst into Boase's office whilst hurriedly putting on his coat.

'Boase, she's been spotted. Someone tipped us off in St Blazey – saw someone they thought was her going into a caravan after visiting a grocery shop. If it's her, she didn't go far.'

'Well, we should go – she might be planning to go upcountry at any moment.'

'Yes – come on.'

Bolton, Boase, Coad and Eddy bundled into two cars and headed towards St Blazey. Boase drove the first car, Eddy followed.

Bolton looked at Boase.

'Do you know this area at all, Boase?'

'Fortunately like the back of my hand, Sir.'

'Oh? How so?'

Boase grinned.

'Did my training at Par before I went to France. Horrible it was. Frozen half to death, we all hated it. They wanted us to be fit for war, then when we got there, after a couple of weeks, we'd run out of food, half of us were dead, the other half, including me, lice-ridden and starving and berated because we had all grown beards – fact was, we had no razor blades. Oh yes, I know the area all right...ran around most of the streets in Par, Tywardreath, St Blazey – I was with such a good bunch of chaps. Most of them never even got brought home. What an unspeakable outrage.'

Boase stopped talking. They had just got to the town of St Austell and he felt he had said enough. He rarely spoke about the war, even tried not to think about it. Sometimes, even now, he'd wake up sweating, shouting – a couple of times crouching under the bed. These things he never spoke of to anyone – he felt it a weakness and that he should have got over it by now.

The two cars reached the top of St Blazey and they pulled over to the side of the road.

'Where now, Sir?'

'Well apparently, the caravan is situated on St Andrew's Road – know where that is?'

'I certainly do.'

'Boase turned the car down a side road and after about half a mile, they reached a railway crossing.

'This is St Andrew's Road, Sir.'

'Right – drive along here and look out for a caravan.'

After about two hundred yards the road widened and a small group of caravans could be seen.

'Right, Boase – keep driving on, we'll leave the cars and walk back. We don't want to alert her if she's here.'

'I hope your informant was correct, Sir – that it's her.'

'Seemed fairly certain. We'll see.'

After about a minute, Boase turned the car left into a narrow road named Driving Lane. He pulled over, got out of the car and indicated to Eddy to do the same.

Bolton pulled his collar up higher.

'I hope she's here.'

'Hold your nerve, Sir.'

The four men made the short walk back along St Andrews Road. As they neared the caravans, Bolton directed them into pairs.

'Right, we're not going to do anything yet – just watch and see if anything happens. She may have an accomplice – but at the very least, someone who is prepared to help her.'

The four men, in pairs, stood amongst the shrubbery, hardly daring to move or even blink in case they missed something. Boase could feel his feet going to sleep as the sun went down and the temperature dropped. A light came on in one of the caravans. The others were in darkness and appeared unoccupied.

'Ready yet, Sir?'

'Just a moment. Someone's definitely in there – let's hope it's her. Okay. Go!'

The four men moved swiftly towards the caravan. Bolton opened the door – it wasn't even locked. He and Boase entered the small caravan while Coad and Eddy went around the back. Just as Bolton realised the caravan was now empty, Coad and Eddy were staring at him through the gaping hole that had been the window. The entire window had carefully been removed and it seems, facilitated the occupant's escape. Boase's shoulders visibly sank. Bolton ran out of the caravan and around to the back.

'Right – all of you, that light only came on less than ten minutes ago. She must have realised we were here. She can't have gone far – go after her!'

The four men separated and suddenly, the light was gone. They all lit their torches. Boase, leaving the others, ran into the woods behind the caravans. He ran for two or three minutes then stopped at a clearing. He listened. Not a sound and then a twig snapped. Boase turned and was dealt a sharp blow to the side of the head. He fell to the ground.

Twenty minutes passed and a light rain began to fall. Bolton had met up with the other two.
'Any sign of Boase?'
'No, Sir.'
Eddy pointed in the direction of the woods.
'He went that way when he left us.'
'Come on then. I think if he'd found anything he would have whistled – that's why I got a bit worried.'
The three made their way through the woodland and came to the clearing. It was empty. They shone their torches about – not a sign of anything. They separated and began to call for Boase.
'Oi – what's goin' on? What's all the noise?'
As the policemen turned to look at who was addressing them, they saw a shabby man, tramp-like in appearance approaching them.
'What's all this carry on, I'd like to know?'
Bolton shone his torch at the man who promptly covered his eyes with his hands.
'Who are you, man – what are you doing here?'
'I live 'ere – I might ask you the same.'
'Have you seen a young man around here?'
'As it 'appens, yes, I 'ave. 'e's over this way.'
The man led the way across the clearing and the others followed. They came to a small stone built building. The man went inside and invited the guests. They found themselves in a tiny room where a fire blazed in the grate. In the corner, Boase was sitting on a small stool, holding a rag to his head. Bolton went over to him.
'You all right, Boase? What happened?'
'I'm not sure – but I'm okay, thanks.'

The old man came forward into the middle of the room.

'I went out to get some more wood for the fire and I saw this young man lying on the ground – I think 'e was unconscious. I sat with him until 'e came round then I managed to get him back 'ere and tend to him. I gave 'im a cuppa and cleaned 'is 'ead. Looks like 'e 'ad quite a knock.'

'Well, thank you – I'm greatly indebted to you, much obliged indeed. We'll be on our way now and leave you in peace. But – I don't suppose you've seen a middle-aged woman around here lately, have you?'

'I can't say I 'ave – no. I'm sorry.'

'No matter – thank you for what you've done for Boase. Good night.'

'The four made their way back through the woods, Boase still holding the rag to his wound.

'Coad, wait here on the road with Boase - I'll go with Eddy to get the cars.'

'No, Sir, it's fine. I can walk to the car.'

'Well, you can't drive, I'll do it.'

'Thank you, Sir.'

The four arrived back at the cars. As Boase was about to get into the passenger side, he looked up at the large house known as Trescowe, which stood on the corner of St Andrews Road and Driving Lane. A woman was up on the garden wall, staring right at him. He reached into his pocket for his torch and directed the beam onto her face. Realising she had been seen, the woman darted back into the bushes.

'She's there – in that garden!'

Bolton, already in the car, flung open the door and ran across the road. Coad and Eddy followed.

'Boase, wait under this wall – mind she doesn't jump down.'

The other three ran around the edge of the wall until they came to a gate which opened and led them up into the garden and to the front of the house.

Bolton whispered to the other two.

'Eddy, you wait by the gate, block this exit. Coad, come with me.'

As he spoke, a noise came from the bushes and without instruction or warning, Coad had pounced like a cat on a mouse. A loud shriek followed.

'Got her, Sir. She's here – I've got her.'

The woman struggled as Coad put handcuffs on her.

'Let me go! I said, let me go.'

'I'm sorry, madam, but we're taking you back to Falmouth. What a merry dance you've led us.'

Bolton put Esme Shepherd into the back of car with Coad next to her.

'And don't try any funny business.'

Boase smiled. That was what Bartlett always used to say. The two cars arrived back at Falmouth and the prisoner was settled into a cell for the night.

'Boase, we'll deal with her tomorrow. I have no energy left in me tonight.'

'Right, Sir. See you tomorrow. Night.'

Boase couldn't sleep. He got out of bed, dressed and went down to the kitchen. He looked into a small mirror; he had a large gash on the side of his head which was now congealed blood. He was thankful that it had stopped bleeding. He took a pocket handkerchief and, after running it under the cold tap, held it to the wound. The coolness soothed the burning almost immediately and he repeated the procedure. He found a couple of fruit buns in the pantry and stuffed them into his pocket. He pulled on his coat and boots and set off for the sea front. He had a headache and hoped the fresh night air would help.

Boase couldn't understand about Villiers and the Fletcher prize. He racked his brains over why that might be relevant – possibly it wasn't. He had heard that Villiers was in industry, and very wealthy. Why had the Beauforts taken exception to him? Because he was married probably – or maybe they knew something else.

At half past four in the morning, Boase returned to his bed. His headache was slightly better and he slept until half past six. Arriving at the police station, he walked through the front door two minutes after Superintendent Bolton.
'Good morning, Boase – how's the head?'
'Bit better thanks, Sir.'
'She must have hit you quite hard by the look of that. Want to go up the hospital?'
'No thanks, Sir – I've seen enough of that place to last me a lifetime.'
'Yes, I should think you probably have. Right, apparently our prisoner has eaten her breakfast so get us a cuppa and we'll go and talk to her.'

Bolton and Boase sat in a side room with Esme Shepherd. She drank a cup of tea as they talked.
'If you don't confess to what we think you've done, we do have a woman who can identify you.'
'I haven't done anything wrong...'
Bolton spoke as Boase listened and made notes.
'That's not what we've heard. We've heard that you have been assisting women in getting rid of their unwanted pregnancies. That's against the law – you must know this?'
'Well, let me tell you this – you and your law. I was a nurse. I worked in London. Some of my patients who came to me for help were very wealthy, influential, well respected, but,

well, anyone can make a mistake, anyone can find themselves in a spot of bother. Some of the other women who came to me were poor. They didn't want rid of their children because it would disgrace their husband who was a member of parliament – or the Lord of the Manor. No! They were women who had nothing. They might have already had six, eight even fifteen children already, yes, children they couldn't feed – children they couldn't clothe. Another mouth to try to put food into. And then, the old man comes back from the pub, drunk again, spending the money that, by rights, is for those poor children. And then his wife asks how much he's spent – then he hits her once or twice, then attacks her in a way that no man ever should. A few weeks later she's coming to me distraught, absolutely beside herself with another on the way. You men have no idea, no idea what it's like.'

'Well, yes, I think you've made it very clear, however, the fact remains that you have been performing illegal acts which have resulted in death. Would you care to comment on that?'

'Yes. Yes I would care to comment on that. For every one that goes wrong, I've had ten or fifteen very happy women – grateful, grateful they were to be out of the mess.'

'Well, you've been a very foolish woman and I have to tell you you're going to be in a lot of trouble.'

Bolton, visibly upset by the woman's seemingly carefree attitude, left the room and Boase took her back to her cell. The desk sergeant came up to him as he returned through the lobby.

'Courier just left this for you or the chief.'

He handed Boase a large brown package. Boase took it to his office and tore it open. He was expecting this today. He read the contents. It was confirming that a box of chocolates found in Esme Shepherd's house had contained thallium. Boase didn't know if this was good news or not. What now?

He wasn't really any further on with this news. He went to tell Bolton.

Esme Shepherd was told that she would have to stay at the Falmouth police station for two more days and then she would be removed to Exeter. Boase felt there was something more she could tell but he couldn't quite figure out what else she knew. He resolved to speak to Bartlett that same evening and to update him with the latest news.

Irene answered the door. She was becoming more confident and assertive with each passing day and had made it known to her parents that she needed to do more for herself. As the door opened, Boase felt his breath was almost taken away. He felt that every time he saw Irene she was more beautiful than the last. He didn't speak, not wanting to break that moment. He looked at her in her oldest dress, green paisley which she always said she hated and what was she thinking of when she had bought it…on top was a shabby brown long woollen cardigan which she had knitted for herself when she was a teenager. Her growing hair was pulled up into a high, untidy bun and held in place with a small, floral clip. It was still wispy where it was growing back and thin tendrils fell about her face. The pomander he had given her was around her neck and she fiddled with it a little nervously, the visitor having the advantage.

'Irene, it's me.'

'Oh, Archie, why didn't you say so, instead of just standing there and making me worried?'

'I'm so sorry, Irene, I didn't mean to upset you…I was just a little surprised that you had come to the door.'

He felt a little foolish to say that he was once more so overcome with her beauty that for a moment he couldn't speak.

'I'm blind – not dead you silly man. Are you coming in or staying on the step all evening?'

She held the door open and Boase stepped into the hall. He kissed her cheek and, in return, she kissed him on his mouth.

'Dad's in here – I suppose it's him not me you've come to see?'

'I always want to see you, Irene – but, yes, I do need to speak to him if that's all right?'

'I'll be in the kitchen with Mum – we're baking.'

Boase went into the dining room where Bartlett was reading the *Falmouth Packet* which he had spread out on the dining table.

'You must like it here, Boase.'

'I'm so sorry to trouble you again, Sir.'

'That's perfectly all right – I was only joking. We're always pleased to see you, you know that. God, man – what have you done to your head?'

At that point, Irene was passing the door and heard her father's comment. She came into the dining room.

'What's happened, Archie?'

'Oh, nothing really – just got a bang on the head, it's okay now.'

'Are you all right – who did that to you? Is it bad?'

Irene had tears in her eyes – upset that she couldn't see the damage done to Archie.

'Irene, it's fine – nothing that a cup of tea won't make better.'

'I thought you might like a beer?'

'Sir, it's only half past six…'

'Didn't know there was a time limit on it now?'

Irene giggled.

'Look, I'll make some tea – I'm quite good at that now, aren't I, Dad? Maybe you could have some beer a bit later if you're still here, Archie?'

That sounds like a good idea – thank you, Irene.'

'So, why did she go to St Blazey?'
Bartlett and Boase had moved into the parlour and Bartlett was tapping his pipe on the fireplace.
'Well, I don't know – but someone saw her. I don't know who but we have been showing her picture around quite a bit. Anyway, they were right and we've got her now.'
'Strange sort of business this is, my boy. And you say she was also poisoned with chocolates?'
'Yes, Turkish Delight.'
'Just the same as Irene…shhh…here she comes with the tea.'
'Can you manage, Irene, dear?'
Boase leapt from his chair as Irene paused with the tray for a moment. He took the tray from her.
'It's all right, Archie, thank you. I just need to get my bearings sometimes.'
Boase set the tray down on a small table.
'Are you having tea, Irene?'
'No, thank you – I'm still helping Mum, well, hindering probably. You chat with Dad.'
'I don't mind admitting to you Boase, I'm well and truly stumped. What a strange set of circumstances. And what of Villiers? Why is he on your mind?'
'I don't rightly know about him – just feel something's not right.'
Boase stayed on until ten o'clock and chatted with Irene and Caroline. He walked home, feeling rather tired due to the previous late night, and the couple of bottles of beer.

Chapter Sixteen

Doris Pellow felt sick. She hadn't got over the recent attack in Market Street. She had been back to Bell's Court to thank the people who had helped her – possibly saved her life but she hadn't been to the police. Now she felt bad. What if that horrible man attacked someone else? Or maybe it was just her he wanted to hurt. He could have murdered her – in which case she must tell the police. What had he meant – that she might already know him from somewhere else? She only knew him as the man who visited his wife in the asylum, usually at the same time she was there visiting her father. She thought – she knew his face very well and she would know him again, but only from those few visits when she had observed him sitting talking to his poor wife. She had told Iris Harcourt what had happened – well, she had no choice anyway when she had been carried back to the flat in such a state and when Iris had to make excuses for her at work.

Doris didn't know what to do for the best. She couldn't put out of her mind what that man had said – about her knowing her from elsewhere. She was so sure she didn't – and she was good with remembering faces usually. Iris had tried to encourage her to go to the police station, even offered to go with her but Doris had remained firm. What if he found out she had told them – what then? He might come for her again. No, she had stood her ground and flatly refused to tell anyone, whilst swearing Iris to secrecy. But maybe now was the time to say something – just in case he did that to anyone else.

Boase left work earlier than usual the next day, at three o'clock to be precise. He went into a café for some tea and a sandwich then, crossing the Moor, went into the Passmore Edwards public library.

'Yes, we do have old copies of the Falmouth Packet. What date were you looking for?'

The young librarian looked at Boase enquiringly.

'Well, Miss, I think I'm looking for nineteen hundred and two.'

'Come with me, I'll take you to the reading room.'

Boase followed the girl across the lobby and into another room which seemed to be populated with old men reading newspapers.

'Wait here please, I'll see what I can find for you.'

'You're very kind. Thank you.'

The girl returned with a box of papers and laid them onto a large mahogany table.

'Is there anything in particular you're looking for?'

'I'm not quite sure, but I'll just look through if that's all right with you?'

'Of course – come and see me if you need anything else.'

Boase took off his coat and sat at the large table. He began his search. By half past four the young woman returned. Boase stood up from his seat.

'Sorry to interrupt, please sit down – I just wanted to remind you that we close at five o'clock.'

'Thank you, Miss.'

Boase hadn't found anything of interest here. He muttered to himself under his breath.

'One more…then I'll finish.'

As he turned one more page, he couldn't believe what he saw. There looking up at him from the page was Edgar Villiers, nineteen hundred and two winner of the Fletcher prize for chemistry. Boase sat back down in his seat and began to read the article. It said that local man Edgar Villiers, son of the eminent industrial chemist, Nathaniel Villiers, had been awarded the Fletcher prize for chemistry in relation to his research. Boase continued to read. The young librarian had returned and was beginning to close the rooms up. Boase returned the papers to their original folders and, thanking the young woman for her help, put on his coat and hat and left the building. It was almost five o'clock and Boase was quite tired. He returned home, pleased and excited with his findings.

Doris Pellow sat on the seat in the lobby of the Falmouth police station. She nervously looked at her watch – it was ten past nine. A door leading from the lobby opened and Boase stood there.

'Miss Pellow – would you like to come in?'

Boase offered Doris a seat in his office.

'Would you like some tea?'

'No – thank you, I can't really be long, I have to be at work.'

'How can I help you?'

Doris retold the tale of what had happened to her the night she was attacked. She explained that she knew who the assailant was and about the assistance she had received. She went on to tell Boase about the visits to her father in the asylum and the man she had seen there and then again in the café.

'Why didn't you say before, Miss?'

'Because I was frightened – I still am but my friend persuaded me to come and tell you in case it was important but, more, in case he did this to someone else.'

'Well, your friend was right. So, you know who this man is? You could identify him?'

'Yes – I could, and I think his name is, well it's a funny name, but I think it's Mr Villiers.'

'Villiers?'

'Yes, that's right – I've heard them at the asylum talking to him and his wife, Mr and Mrs Villiers they call them.'

'Are you absolutely sure?'

'Yes.'

'And this was at the asylum over on the Redruth road?'

'That's right – Meadowbank. But...'

'...but what?'

'Well it's all rather strange really. When he attacked me from behind – it was only when he spoke and what he said that I realised who he was.'

At that point, Boase pulled a notebook from the desk drawer.

'What did he say?'

'It was something like "if I should see you again when I'm visiting my wife, don't even look at me, do you understand?" Then he said to me "if you remember where else you've seen me, and if you try to tell anyone, you will be in deep trouble, I give you my word." That's what he said.'

Have you seen him somewhere else? Can you remember?'

'I keep thinking over and over – I don't think so. I've tried so hard but I don't think I know him from anywhere else.'

'All right, Miss. Leave this with me. Thank you for coming in to see me. Be sure to leave your address at the front desk in case I need to contact you again.'

'I will – thank you for listening.'

In his confusion over the story he had just heard, Boase had almost forgotten what he had discovered the previous day in the library. He knocked on Superintendent Bolton's door.

'I found out something interesting yesterday, Sir.'

'What's that then? Sit down, Boase.'

Boase closed the door behind him and sat down.

'Yesterday I went to the library – I had something on my mind since a conversation with Penhaligon, something that didn't sit quite right about Edgar Villiers. I trawled through some old papers and found out something. It seems Mr Edgar Villiers isn't all he seems.'

'Oh? Go on.'

'Well, we just thought he was a wealthy businessman with an inheritance – turns out there's more to him than meets the eye. His father was Nathaniel Villiers. Apparently he was an industrial chemist and remarkably good at what he did. Seems he set up factories and provided employment in and around Prussia in the seventies and eighties. It all came crashing down when he was found to be supplying weapons to a small group setting themselves up to bring down the establishment – he shot himself in the foot, so to speak, when he did that. Very clever man but not clever enough not to get caught. Anyway, Edgar Villiers is actually a research chemist as well as a businessman. It would appear though that he can't let go of his work.'

'What do you mean?'

'Well, in nineteen hundred and two, Villiers the younger was awarded the Fletcher prize for chemistry in recognition of the work he had built upon which was previously conducted by two men named Crookes and Lamy.'

'What did they do in the great war?'

Boase smiled, that was something Bartlett always used to say.

Crookes and Lamy didn't work together – one was English, the other, French. In 1862 they, independently of each other, discovered a new chemical element and Villiers was later awarded the prize for further research on that element.'

'What has this got to do with us?'
'The element was thallium, Sir.'
'You jest!'
'Absolute truth, Sir. I just had a bad feeling about him all along and you know when sometimes you can't see what it is that's playing on your mind?'
This is unbelievable – this can't be a coincidence, can it?'
'Well, if it is, it's a big one. Something else happened this morning too.'
'What?'
'A young woman came in here first thing to make a complaint that she had been attacked, going back a few weeks now but she was afraid to tell us because she had been threatened. Her attacker, as far as I can understand, was Edgar Villiers.'
'This is just getting more and more complicated now, Boase. What do we do next? What do you recommend?'
Boase, whilst flattered that the Superintendent was asking a constable how to proceed, felt that it wasn't his place to advise on this.
'I don't really know, Sir. What do you think?'
'I suppose we find Villiers and question him. That would be a start – I don't see how he could have managed to do all this…and what was his motive?'
'I suppose only he can tell us that. I have his address, I'll take Rabone and go over there.'

At eleven o'clock, Boase and Rabone drove over to Helford Passage and parked outside the grand waterfront house owned by Edgar Villiers. Boase knocked on the door. No reply came. Rabone went around the back of the house but the only gate allowing admittance was firmly locked. Boase came round to the back just in time to see Rabone unsuccessfully trying to scale the gate and falling spectacularly into a holly bush. Boase laughed loudly.

'You're such a plank, Rabone.'

The two retraced their steps and went around to the other side of the house. A small window next to a glazed door had been carelessly left open and the key sitting in the lock was within reach.

'Can you get your arm through there, Rabone?'

'I'll give it a try.'

Rabone stretched up and carefully reached in through the open window. From there he just about reached the key.

'Don't know if I can turn it. It's just out of reach.'

'Hang on, I'll give you a leg-up.'

Boase lifted Rabone up. Rabone being the bigger-framed man made this a struggle.

'Be quick, I'm dropping you!'

The key turned and Boase, almost collapsing under the strain, let Rabone down.

'You need to eat fewer pasties!'

Rabone looked at Boase.

'Well, if there was any justice, I'd eat as much as you do and be like a rake.'

Boase had opened the door and the two went in. He motioned to Rabone to look upstairs. The house was quiet and all the curtains were still drawn closed. Boase entered the sitting room. The curtains were drawn back in here and sunlight was filtering through. It was a large room with windows the whole width of it and with views stretching right up the Helford river. On one side was a bookcase. Boase picked up one or two of the books – they were almost all to do with science. On a small table was a writing case and a lady's manicure set. A few flowery china ornaments indicated that this must be Mrs Villiers' own table. Boase wondered what had happened to her. All he knew was that she was in a home for the insane. Suddenly he heard a loud crash from upstairs. He ran back out into the hall and called out.

'Rabone – what was that?'

'Sorry, something fell off the wardrobe when I opened it. No damage done. There's no one about up here.'

'Same down here.'

Boase opened another door which brought him into a very large kitchen. He looked about. There was a large range at one end and a big table in the middle. He thought about Irene. How she would love a kitchen like this. She loved to cook and entertain. He wished he could give her something like this, but even if he could, would she ever see it? He left the kitchen, closing the door behind him. Crossing the hall again, he entered into a very grand dining room. This room was in near darkness, the curtains still being shut. He was now at the back of the house, the sitting room no doubt having the best river views.

Boase walked to the window. There was a small half-moon table to one side with smoking paraphernalia on it. Boase picked up a pipe that was inlaid with mother-of-pearl; he couldn't imagine George Bartlett using anything like this. He walked back across the room and to the door. He stopped. He thought. Why was no one here? Where was Villiers? Was there no housekeeper? He returned to the window and pulled back the curtain.

'Rabone…RABONE! Come here.'

As Rabone came running down the stairs he bumped into Boase in the hall.

'Quickly, come into the garden. He's there!'

The two policemen ran outside and to the lawn. Villiers was face down on the grass. Boase turned him over. He had cuts to his wrists – but he was alive.

'There's a telephone in the hall, Rabone. Get help – quickly!'

Boase pulled a handkerchief from his pocket and removed his scarf from about his neck. Moving swiftly, he bandaged the man's wrists. The man groaned.

'Villiers...Villiers. Wake up man! Hey...wake up!'

Villiers opened his eyes then closed them again. Boase patted his face.

'Come on – don't do this to me...wake up, come on.'

Rabone returned to the garden.

'There was a telephone pad on the table – I managed to get hold of the village doctor, he's on his way. Should we take him to hospital?'

'Let's wait for the doctor. He doesn't look that bad - he's a bit pale but I don't think he's lost much. Keep talking to him, I'll wait at the entrance for the doctor.'

Boase waited at the end of the drive and soon the doctor appeared in his car. Boase led the way to the house and into the garden. The doctor tended to the man.

'Why do people do this to themselves? Look I've given him an injection and he needs to go to hospital to be taken care of. He'll live. Can you take him into Falmouth?'

'Yes, Doctor, we can take him now. Thank you for coming out so promptly.'

'That's all right, don't delay now.'

The doctor scribbled something which appeared illegible on a piece of paper and handed it to Boase.

'Give this to the doctor who admits him – it'll tell him what I've done.'

'I will. Thank you, Doctor.'

Boase and Rabone carried the man to the car. He was still in and out of consciousness but better than before. By the time they reached the Falmouth Hospital, he was able to walk, aided, into the building. Boase explained to the doctor what had happened and that he would like to come back later to talk to Villiers as he was a suspect in their case. He added that he would be sending a policeman immediately to make sure this one didn't get away.

Boase relayed to Bolton what had happened and immediately despatched a constable to watch Villiers at the hospital.
'Why would he do that, Boase?'
'Dunno, Sir. Guilty conscience? I'm going back up there tomorrow morning, the doctor will have assessed him then and he told me I could speak to him.'
'Want me to come?'
'It's okay, Sir, I can manage this one.'

Boase called by the Bartlett's house that evening.
'Shall we put a bed up for you in the parlour, Boase?'
'Sorry, Sir.'
'I'm joking – anyway, I asked you to keep me abreast of events. What's the latest?'
Boase explained what had happened with Edgar Villiers and about his expert knowledge of thallium. He explained that he was going to interview him in the morning.
'Sounds too much of a coincidence that's he's not your man. But why?'
'That's what Bolton said. Maybe it'll all become clear tomorrow when I speak to him.'
'Wish I was coming with you.'
'Oh, so do I, Sir. I miss having you around – you're always so sensible.'
'I don't know about that but, well we do think alike and get on quite well, wouldn't you say?'
'Yes. Yes, I would say. Are you ever coming back, Sir?'
'I don't think they want me back, my boy.'

'But Bolton is only temporary – we need you back.'

'I'll wait and see what happens. The girls like having me around the house but, between us, it's driving me mad. I don't feel old enough to be put out to grass just yet. Oh, I almost forgot – this might interest you. It was in my newspaper today. Wait – now, where did I put my reading spectacles?'

'They're in your breast pocket, Sir.'

'Oh, so they are. I'm such an old fool sometimes. Now listen to this.'

Bartlett put on his reading glasses and read to Boase from the paper.

'It says here about your woman, Esme Shepherd. Says that she's confessed to everything. Listen - says a bit of preamble about her first then this –

"Esme Shepherd moved to Falmouth from London where she had been a nurse for many years. With a legacy from a maiden aunt, she managed to secure shares in several eating establishments in Falmouth, including the Mermaid, George's Café and The Rose Tearooms. These same establishments are the subject of ongoing investigations by the local police in connection with a series of poisonings resulting in much sickness and at least two fatalities. This woman now also stands accused of carrying out illegal acts thought to number around two hundred resulting in illness, severe trauma and possibly two dozen fatalities." What do you make of that?'

'That's unbelievable, Sir.'

'Isn't it just?'

'Anyway, look, I won't hold you up any longer. Where's Irene?'

'That's all right, Boase. Irene has gone to a music recital or something with a friend. A girl, I might add before you start getting any silly ideas in your head. Do you remember her speaking about an old friend from her school days, Dot Cameron? She's a photographer or something now, very

Bohemian type. She's staying in the town for a few days and she called on Irene on Thursday. They had remained friends, well pen-pals you might say. She didn't know why Irene had stopped communicating with her. She was shocked to discover what had happened but then, obviously, realised why Irene had stopped writing. Anyway, she has a car and the pair went off together earlier this afternoon.'

'That's nice for her.'

'Yes, we're all trying to encourage her – and to get back to normal, well, as normal as possible.'

'Right – I'll keep you posted, Sir. Bye for now.'

'Please do. Bye, Boase.'

Chapter Seventeen

'Sir, do you think there would be any chance of visiting Esme Shepherd in Exeter?'

Bolton looked up from his paperwork.

'Why on earth would you want to do that, Boase? I should think you'd be glad to see the back of that awful woman – she's a piece of work, and a menace.'

'Well, yes, I know – but don't you think she's the only person that could tell us if there's a connection between her and Villiers?'

'Villiers could tell you?'

'Well, yes, but I don't trust him. He could lie to us. She has nothing to lose and I would hope that she might do the right thing now.'

'It's possible – maybe. But she's out of our jurisdiction now.'

Bolton admired the ways Boase had of problem solving – he was certainly lucky to have him at the moment. George Bartlett had taught him well.

'Well, why don't you see Villiers first – see how you get on?'

'Right, Sir. But if he won't tell us anything…'

'Don't try to second guess it – see what happens.'

The doctors at the Falmouth Hospital had delayed any communication with Edgar Villiers on the basis that they felt he wasn't well enough. Boase was angry – this was just wasting more time unnecessarily. Two days had passed and he was unable to see him. Eventually Superintendent Bolton received a call.

'Boase – we've just had a telephone call from the hospital…you can go and see him at three o'clock.'

Boase arrived at half past two and waited in the hospital lobby. At five minutes to three a nurse invited him in to see Edgar Villiers. The patient was half sitting up in his bed. Boase noticed the bandages on his wrists. He pulled up a chair next to the bed and introduced himself.

'I think you've been expecting me. I need to talk to you.'

'What is there to talk about?'

'Plenty. First of all, why did you do this to yourself?'

'Why not, I'm tired of everything, Constable Boase. My life is hard, the woman I love is dead…'

'…but your wife is still alive?'

Villiers half smiled.

'I mean Topsy. I loved her and now she's gone. My wife will never come out of that place, I have no one.'

'What were you trying to run away from?'

'What makes you think I was running away from anything? If you hadn't turned up, I wouldn't be here now.'

What do you know of a young woman by the name of Doris Pellow?'

'Never heard of her.'

'She's the woman you attacked in Bell's Court – don't say it wasn't you. Why did you do that?'

'I did nothing, I know no one of that name. She doesn't even sound like someone I would want to know.'

'Well, foolishly, you made yourself known to her by what you said. You must have known she'd tell us?'

'I told her not…'

'…not to say anything? Yes, that's what she told me.'

Villiers scowled.

'So why did you attack her?'

'I didn't attack her – she was following me up the street, I didn't like the way she always looked at me when I was visiting my wife. I told her to stop. She ran off and fell. I never touched her. And no, I didn't know her name.'

'I'm sorry – I don't believe your story. I'm going to be asking you to come to the police station for further questioning when you leave here. I will have a man here to bring you so don't try running off.'

'Do what you like, see if I care.'

'What do you know about Esme Shepherd?'

'Who?'

Boase was really beginning to dislike this man – pretending he was so stupid when actually he was a very clever man.'

'You heard – Esme Shepherd. She used to be a nurse in London, lives here now. Know her?'

'No.'

'Right Mr Villiers – thank you for your time. I'll be seeing you again very soon.'

Boase spoke to the doctor treating Edgar Villiers and he confirmed that the patient would be discharged in two days' time.

At eight o'clock the next morning, Doris Pellow and Iris Harcourt were walking along Market Street on their way to work at the Rose Tearooms. They stopped at the entrance to the Prince of Wales pier.

'Doris, I want to buy some oranges to take to work. I know we can have lunch there but sometimes, well, it's just nice to have a piece of fruit to eat when we get a break.'

'Yes, it is. Go into Jennings and get some then – will you get a couple for me, here, I'll give you the money, I just want to walk over to the pier.'

Doris opened her bag and took some money from her purse. She handed it to Iris.

'Get me a couple of apples too, please.'

'Right, will do. Wait over there for me.'

Doris walked onto the pier. Below her she could see the Mermaid. It was now open for business again. She looked across the water to Flushing. Suddenly a thought came to her mind and she felt rather unwell. She sat on the pier steps for a moment for fear of falling. She felt all of a sudden very hot, her face flushed and a pain came to her chest. Now she couldn't breathe. Iris came over to her carrying two bags of fruit. She looked for Doris but couldn't see her. Running on to the pier, she caught sight of the familiar red cardigan. She ran to the steps.

'What are you doing here? I couldn't find you.'

Looking at Doris, she dropped the fruit down on the step.

'What's the matter? Doris, what's happened?'

At that, Doris leaned forward and vomited into the water.

'Oh, Iris, forgive me, I'm so sorry.'

'Can you walk? Are you able to stand up? Come on – I'll take you home. What is it? Have you eaten something bad?'

'I don't think so. Just the faggots we had last night – and Mr Mannell is always so good with the meat he sells. No, I don't think it's anything I ate. I was all right when we came out but then suddenly I just started thinking about things and felt really upset. I think I'd like to go home please, if you could help me. I...I feel a bit unsteady.'

Iris helped her friend up from the steps and handed her her bag. Picking up the bags of fruit, she held Doris's arm and they walked slowly back to their flat.

Doris lay on the sofa and Iris fetched a cool flannel for her head.

'You feeling any better, now, dear?'

'A little, thank you. I don't know what happened – one minute I was fine, the next…'

'Well you have a little colour back now, thankfully. Can I get you anything?'

'Maybe some water, please.'

As Iris returned with the water, Doris sat up.

'Iris, do you remember that man that came around selling stuff a while back. He had chocolates and sweets?'

'Not sure, why?'

'Yes you do – you said he was quite a dish and I said he was an old man who looked like he'd put boot polish on his hair to hide his age?'

'Oh, yes, yes, I remember now. I thought he was rather handsome, no, distinguished. Why?'

'I think he's the man who attacked me.'

'No! How could that possibly be? Why would you even think that? You didn't see the man who attacked you, you told me that.'

'No, I didn't see him, but he said things that made me recognise him. I know who he is – I told you. He's the man who has an insane wife over at the place where Dad is.'

Well, yes, you did tell me that. But what are you getting at, Doris, dear? Are you sure you're quite well?'

'Yes. I'm well. I'm asking you about the commercial traveller because I think he is also the same man. The man from the asylum, the man who attacked me and the commercial traveller.'

'My, he's a busy person then.'

'Don't you see what I'm saying, Iris – what this means?'

'To be honest, no, I don't. Maybe you're just overtired. Why don't you go to bed?'

'Why don't you ever listen?'

Iris stared at her friend. This was an uncommon outburst indeed.

'Oh! Iris, I'm so sorry – please accept my apology. Yes, you're right. I'm probably sickening for something. I think I will go and have a little nap for an hour. Perhaps I'll feel better after that.

'I think that might be a very good idea. Can I bring you anything back later?'

'No – but please can you deal with work for me?'

'Yes, don't even worry about that – I'll tell them what happened. It'll be fine.'

Boase was so angry, he couldn't sleep. He sat up in bed thinking about his interview with Villiers. Why was he doing this? First he admitted a crime and now, well now he wouldn't give anything and Boase had nowhere to go. He had the know-how on the thallium – but then, what could be his motive? Maybe he enabled someone else to plant the poison? He really needed to pay a visit to Esme Shepherd – maybe appeal to her for her help; that could go either way he thought to himself. She might dig in her heels and say nothing. He'd speak to Bolton in the morning – he would be forceful and insist that he permitted Boase to visit. He tried to lay down and sleep but just became more and more angry. When he couldn't sleep as a child his mother used to tell him to think of nice things – the only nice thing he could think of right now was Irene. Since everything that had happened to her, he had realised just how much she had meant to him. Truth be told, he blamed himself for the events – if he hadn't been so foolish about her hair, if he had been a bit more grown up and reasonable then she would have stayed with him, she wouldn't have been poisoned. Yes, he had been such an idiot and now he owed it to her to see the person who had hurt her so terribly be found and brought to justice. He would solve this. He'd do it for Irene.

As Boase sat at his desk eating a cheese sandwich, Penhaligon came into the office.

'I'm sorry to interrupt, but there's a young woman out here asking for you.'

'Who is it?'

'She says her name is Doris Pellow.'

'Oh – okay, give me a minute.'

Boase swept the crumbs from his shirt, pushed the half-eaten sandwich into the desk drawer and pulled his jacket from the back of his chair. He put on the jacket and adjusted his cuffs. He went out into the lobby.

'Miss Pellow? Would you like to come in?'

Doris Pellow sat opposite Boase at his desk.

'What brings you here again – I didn't expect another visit?'

'It's about that man – Edgar Villiers.'

'What about him?'

'I've remembered – where else I saw him.'

'*You do?!*'

Yes – I can't believe it took me so long, I've been such a fool.'

'How so?'

'Because I only recognised him as the man from the asylum – that's what I had in my mind. But when I saw him elsewhere, he looked rather different. But now I know and I'm sure of it.'

'Where else did you see him?'

'At my place of work – he came into the Rose Tearooms.'

'He was dining there?'

'No – he was a commercial traveller.'

'Miss Pellow, now you can't seriously expect me to believe that Mr Edgar Villiers, research chemist and wealthy businessman suddenly changed his career and became a salesman. Why on earth would he do that?'

'How should I know? But I told you I'd let you know if I remembered anything else.'

'Yes, yes you did. Thank you. So – what happened when he came into the Rose Tearooms?'

'He asked me if he could see the manager or whoever was in charge of purchasing. So I fetched Mr Simpson.'

'What happened then?'

They both went up to the office – they were up there for about half an hour, then he left.'

'Is Mr Simpson at work today?'

'Yes.'

'I think I need to talk to him. Thank you Miss Pellow, I appreciate you coming in to see me.'

'That's okay – hope it helps. Bye.'

Boase sat at his desk, completely puzzled. What on earth could this mean? She must be mistaken. Nevertheless, he had nothing else to go on, so a visit to Mr Simpson was in order. He had already interviewed the man and had been told that the usual company supplying chocolates had let him down over his order and he saw no harm in trying a different traveller. The salesman had left no calling card and had apparently vanished without trace.

Mr Simpson now sat behind his desk and confirmed exactly the same story this time - no details were left by the traveller. Boase just felt his heart sink – what a blasted fool! That was exactly the same story he had been given by George's and the Mermaid. And he hadn't tied it all in together. He closed his eyes and tried to think back. The Rose Tearooms, George's and the Mermaid; they had all given a new commercial traveller a chance – the Rose Tearooms because they had been let down, the Mermaid, apparently because they had been sold a bad batch of Tartare Sauce in the past and would not entertain the same firm supplying them again and George's Café had never had anyone selling Gentleman's Relish before and thought it would be good to try something different. Oh, for goodness sake! Boase thanked Mr Simpson and left.

Now he also knew that Esme Shepherd was linked to all three places. Boase could kick himself. He hadn't done his job properly when he should have. But he could put it right now. Returning to his office he pulled a notepad from his desk drawer and hastily scribbled a note on one sheet. He put the intended recipient's name on the outside and folded the paper into a makeshift envelope. He paused and thought again. He ripped another sheet from the pad and wrote again, folding it into a similar envelope as the first. He wasn't going to discuss this with Bolton – he felt foolish and he was going to keep this to himself until he had an answer.

Boase ran out into the street – there was a boy standing on the opposite corner, selling newspapers. He ran across to him.
'Hey, boy – deliver these two messages and I'll give you this penny. Make sure you do mind – you can't con a policeman or you'll be arrested.'
'All right – thanks, Mister.'
The boy pushed his newspapers into his bag and ran off at top speed. Boase had a plan now – and he wasn't shifting from it. No more mistakes now.
Bolton left the police station at four o'clock. His mother was seriously ill and asking for him so he had left early and taken twenty-four hours' leave to travel up by train to see her. He had been reluctant under the circumstances but this suited Boase perfectly and he had encouraged the visit to the sick woman. At six o'clock the desk sergeant showed two women into Boase's office.

'Thank you for your time both of you – I'm sorry it's such short notice but I would really appreciate your help.'

Doris Pellow and Alice Hole sat down and listened to what Boase had to say.

'So, I was hoping that if you could describe the traveller who came to you that day – that Alice may be able to sketch your description?'

Doris looked at Alice.

'Well, I can tell you exactly what he looked like.'

'And then I can draw it – I'm sure your description will be good enough to get a likeness.'

'I'll leave you to it, if you like. I can't tell you what a help this will be to me.'

Boase stood on the step outside the police station. He really hoped this would work – but only if the staff at the Mermaid and at George's recognised him from Alice's drawing, and that would only be of real use if it looked like Villiers.

Boase waited almost half an hour and then returned to his office.

'How's it coming along, ladies?'

Alice handed him her finished sketch. Boase couldn't help but admire her skill.

'What do you think, Miss Pellow?'

'It's incredible – it's so life-like, just as he was. I can hardly believe how clever you are, Alice.'

'I can't thank you both enough – you don't know how indebted to you I am.'

The two women left and Boase stared at the sketch. This had to work. Had to work.

Chapter Eighteen

Mrs Villiers, please don't upset yourself. I'm sure your husband will come to see you very soon. Come along now – how about a nice cup of tea? Now, now – don't be like that or you'll have to have one of your pills. Here you are now, have a sip of tea.'

Eunice Villiers had sat in her chair in the window for three days. She had refused to get into bed and just sat waiting for her husband. The Matron held Eunice's hand.

'I'm sure he'll be here soon – he's a very busy man you know. Look, I've even brought one of your favourite biscuits, that always makes you feel better. Come on now, this isn't doing you any good.'

Eunice Villiers drank the tea and ate the biscuit. She leaned back in her chair and closed her eyes.

'You really mustn't spend another night in this chair, Mrs Villiers. Let me help you into bed.'

Eunice pretended to be asleep. The Matron was a very strict nurse and firm but fair, however, she had had a soft spot for Mrs Villiers since the first day she had come to Meadowbank. She hadn't been told of the circumstances of the woman's illness – other than to be told she had had a shock. Nothing more was said other than she was to be admitted as a psychiatric patient. The Matron had seen what Mrs Villiers had seen many times from this window – her husband leaving and crossing the drive, climbing into a very expensive motor car with a young woman – a painted woman the matron had thought. She had even told the nursing sister that she looked like she belonged in a common house of assignation. Yes, she liked Mrs Villiers a lot and felt for her – and she despised her husband, he was a cad. She wrapped a warm blanket around Mrs Villiers' legs and plumped up her pillow. Leaving quietly, she put out the light.

Boase was waiting outside the Rose Tearooms before they even opened. The minute the sign turned over on the door, he entered. He addressed the young waitress who had given him admittance.

'I'd like to speak to Mr Simpson, please, Miss.'

'Just a minute, please, I'll fetch him.'

Mr Simpson slowly descended the stairs from the office.

'Good morning, Mr Simpson.'

'Good morning again, Constable.'

'I want to ask you a question. Is this the man who sold confectionery to you?'

Mr Simpson reached into his pocket for his reading spectacles. Putting them onto the end of his nose, he looked at Alice's sketch.

'Yes, yes, that's the man.'

'Sure?'

'Yes. I cannot tell you any more – I was busy as I recall and I didn't ask for any further particulars. If I remember rightly, I just wanted him to leave as we were beginning to get very busy – it was at about one o'clock.'

'Thank you, Sir – you've been very helpful.'

Boase repeated this visit aboard the Mermaid and at George's. He got the same response – the staff recognised him as the commercial traveller and Boase knew that this was

Villiers. The missing link though was Esme Shepherd. She was associated with these three eateries. Villiers was now associated too. But how did the two of them connect to each other? Boase felt he was getting closer to solving this now.

'Sir, I really need your permission to visit Esme Shepherd – I really think it will help solve the remaining mystery. In fact, I know it will…I don't feel we can go any further without her help.'

'And why should she help us?'

'I'm hoping she'll see it as a final act of charity, to tell us how she's linked to Edgar Villiers. He's denied all knowledge of her – but I don't believe him. He's a nasty piece of work. I think this is the only chance to tie it all up, once and for all.'

'Well, it's not just my permission you'll need – we'd have to clear it with Exeter and they're not the easiest bunch to get along with, I know from previous dealings with them.'

'Please can you try, Sir?'

Superintendent Bolton looked at Boase. He supposed he ought to try – there was something about this young man, he was very good at his job and he needed a break, they all needed a break on this one. He trusted Boase's judgment and for that reason, he agreed.

'I can't promise anything – leave it with me and I'll do my best. But, if they agree, this better be good.'

'Oh, don't worry, Sir, I'm sure it will be.'

Boase left the office wondering what on earth he'd done – he often pushed himself too far but now, well, Esme Shepherd would just have to do the right thing; everything depended on it now. He needed to work quickly – Edgar Villiers was being discharged from the hospital tomorrow evening.

Eunice Villiers had had another bad night. The night sister had come to check on her just in time to see her walking across the landing and towards the stairs. She had made her a hot drink and tried to put her into bed but she still insisted on sitting in the window in her chair. At six o'clock in the morning the Matron came to see her.

'Mrs Villiers, Eunice – how are you feeling? Sister tells me you had a bad night?'

Eunice Villiers didn't speak – she had barely said a word since her admission almost four years ago. She just stared, wide-eyed like a small child, for all the world unaware of what was going on around her – but she did know, she knew exactly; she had seen her husband in her own car that he had bought for her birthday – with that girl. The Matron had felt so sorry for her but thought it best that nothing was said…she had just tried to keep her away from the window when that woman was there.

'Look, I've brought you some breakfast – I know you like to eat early. I've brought you some lovely toast and a boiled egg. I think you ought to have a little something to keep your strength up. Come on now, I'll help you – you'll feel better able to face the day with some food inside you.'

Eunice made a start on a piece of toast then drifted off again as though in a dream.

'Well, you've has a little – well done, good girl. Look, I'll just leave it on your table and you just take some more if you feel like it, all right, dear?'

'Boase – you can visit Esme Shepherd, I've got you your permission. She's in the temporary women's wing at the prison.'

Bolton looked at Boase over the top of his spectacles.

'Better make this one count, then.'

'I will, Sir – thank you. Thank you so much.'

'I suggest you get on the next available train. When is Villiers coming out of hospital?'

'This evening, Sir.'

'Well, I don't know what you're hoping to discover but I wish you luck with it.'

'Yes, Sir – thank you. I'd better make ready to leave.'

Boase, making sure he had plenty of food for his journey, walked to the Falmouth station to wait for his train. After about fifteen minutes he was aboard. The train was quite full and Boase looked out of the window and tried to ignore the chatter going on all about him. He now had a bit of time to think. He pulled his notebook out of his pocket and found a pencil. He jotted down a couple of things he wanted to ask Esme Shepherd. He felt tired – he hoped that today would give him the answers he needed, not only to solve this case once and for all, but to prove to everyone that he was good at his job – he might even get promoted soon and that would be so good…then he could take care of Irene properly and without having to worry about money. Thoughts whirling round and round in his head, Boase leaned against the window and closed his eyes. A child screamed like a parrot in the seat opposite him and he jumped. He stared at the boy who, realising that he had upset his fellow traveller, turned and buried his face in his mother's coat. The mother stared at Boase with a sour look as though he had been the wrongdoer. Forced into a state of alertness by the child, Boase rummaged in his coat pocket. He pulled out a piece of cake and began to eat, now watched again by the child.

The train eventually pulled into Exeter railway station and Boase made his way to the prison. He showed his credentials and explained that he was expected. After being kept waiting for fifteen minutes, he was eventually shown into a room where Esme Shepherd was waiting for him. A prison warden stood at one end of the room. Esme was sitting at a table. Boase pulled up a chair and sat down opposite her.

'You knew I was coming today?'

'Yes – they told me. What do you want?'

'I want you to help me.'

'How can I help you – and more, why should I?'

'I know you've done some bad things, Esme – but I don't believe that you poisoned anyone, indeed, you yourself have been a victim.'

'Just – what do you want?'

Boase reached into his inside coat pocket and pulled out a photograph. He pushed it across the table to Esme.

'Take a look at that.'

The woman picked up the photograph and held it towards the light coming in through a small window.'

'Her name is Irene. She's my girl – we're going to be married, hopefully soon when she's a bit better.'

'She's a very pretty girl – and you're a lucky man. But why are you showing me? Is she unwell?'

'You might say that – she's blind so, yes, I'd call that kind of unwell.'

'Oh, the poor girl – I'm sorry. How long has she been like that?'

'Not very long – just since she ate poisoned chocolates from the Rose Tearooms.'

'Oh no! Oh my word – I'm so sorry.'

'That's why I need your help – other people died at the poisoners' hands – you might say that Irene was lucky but I know for a fact, Mrs Shepherd, that Irene has wished herself dead on more than one occasion.'

'Oh, the poor dear. How terrible for you both.'

'Yes, it's terrible. Look, Mrs Shepherd – what do you know of Edgar Villiers?'

'Why are you asking me about him?'

'So – you know him?'

'Yes, I know him all right. Why – what's he done now?'

'Leave that for a moment, please – tell me what is your connection with him?'

'Well, it goes back a way.'

'Please tell me everything you know.'

'I suppose I have nothing to lose now. He lived in London – as did I. I was a nurse and he, well, he was a chemist or something, I don't know – industrial chemist, along those lines anyway. He had received a prize for his research into something or other – quite important apparently and he was basking in his glory. Anyway, I met him when he was asked to open a new ward in the hospital where I worked. We became friends in a way and he visited the hospital – I think he made regular donations which we were very glad to receive. I met his wife a couple of times – she was a very nice lady, I liked her a lot. Anyway, he confided in me that he had his suspicions that she was having an affair, as I believe they say these days - that she was being unfaithful. He couldn't be sure and I wasn't that interested if I'm honest but, in the end, every time I saw him, it was all he would talk about…almost obsessed he was.

Boase was writing in his notebook. He looked up as a warden came in with two mugs of tea. He put them on the table, without speaking.

'Thank you.'

Boase watched as the man left the room before he spoke.

'Please continue – here, have some tea. Could do with some sugar.'

'You'll be lucky.'

'Indeed. Please carry on.'

'Well, where was I – oh yes, that's right…obsessed he was. Anyway one day he came to me in tears – tears of rage I might add. He said he'd confronted her the night before and she had admitted that she was seeing another man. Worse was to come mind you – she took the opportunity to tell him she was carrying a baby. Well! He pleaded with me to help him…apparently another woman had told him that I helped women out of their difficulties sometimes and he begged me, no, demanded, that I did the same for her. I think this was all about his reputation – quite the lifestyle they had, parties, luncheons, cars, boats – they appeared to have everything except, well, Mrs Villiers obviously felt that she didn't have everything. She often seemed quite lonely and, call it intuition, but I always felt he was chasing around other women while his poor wife was at home alone. She couldn't claim the baby to be his because, well, they hadn't been that way inclined he had confided. Anyway, he persisted until I agreed to see his wife. She was so upset at his suggestion but, he's very domineering, a very unpleasant man and after about three hours, he had finally made her agree – yes, Constable Boase, *made* her agree.

Esme Shepherd paused to sip her tea.

'Anyway – I wasn't really very happy about the whole thing – most women are glad that I can help them but, Mrs Villiers, well, I think she wanted to keep the child. Well, one thing led to another and I did the necessary. Everything went according to plan – she recovered well, physically but it seems that mentally, well, she just fell apart. She got so bad that he left her at home all the time…she was in no fit state to go anywhere or see anyone. A mutual friend told me that for twelve months she just more or less sat in a chair cuddling a child's teddy bear. Eventually I heard that he had taken a job in Cornwall – apparently that's where the family home is…or one of them is. As soon as he got there he had her committed to an asylum, for want of a better word. So, that's really all I can tell you.'

'I'd say that's plenty – as you might imagine, Villiers denied all knowledge of you.'

'I bet he did – now you can see why.'

'Can I just say – you know you told me about the prize he was awarded for his research? That was the Fletcher prize for chemistry in nineteen hundred and two – for his work on the uses of thallium. All of my poisoning incidents were due to thallium.'

'No! Oh my – I can't believe it.'

'So in the light of everything you've just told me, I think Villiers may have blamed you for his troubles and set about destroying you through your businesses – which obviously I know all about – but I couldn't make a link between you and he. I was convinced that he was responsible for all this but I couldn't see a motive – I think now I can and that's the route I'm going to take. Thank you for your help, it means such a lot.'

'I wouldn't have told you any of that or tried to help you in any way – if you hadn't shown me that photograph of your Irene. I'm so sorry – I hope you will be very happy together and mind you take good care of her.'

'I intend to.'

Esme Shepherd patted Boase's hand and stood up.'

'I wish you well, young man, I really do. Be happy and remember, never miss an opportunity.'

The warden led Esme Shepherd to the door. She turned and looked at him once more. Boase felt a little choked – he had seen a different side to the woman he had been pursuing all this time – and maybe she had meant well…and thought she was doing what she did for the best.

It was late in the evening when Boase arrived back at Falmouth. He was tired and a little upset. He couldn't agree with capital punishment, if anything, Boase was a pacifist. He hated what they had all been put through during the war – and for what? For absolutely nothing! Now, it would be a huge surprise if Esme Shepherd was only sentenced to imprisonment – no jury would look favourably on her for this, Boase was sure. He didn't feel comfortable with what she had done, but he had never felt that two wrongs make a right. He went straight home and to bed – he couldn't settle. Esme Shepherd was on his mind all night; if she hadn't helped him and explained the whole story to him, he felt sure this case would have just dragged on and on. He eventually fell asleep at about half past four and woke, un-refreshed, two hours later. He walked to work, feeling like a cloud was hanging over him – he had expected to be happy if he got the information he needed, and to be able to tell Bolton that his actions had paid off. If he was honest, Boase felt bad, almost as though he had used the woman for his own ends. That said, she had done it for Irene – and he must do it for Irene…and see the man who did this to his girl brought to justice.

Superintendent Bolton was sitting behind his desk when Boase knocked and entered.
'Good morning, Boase – Villiers was allowed home last night and I had no reason to arrest him, or even have him watched. How did you get on yesterday?'
'Well, I got a very good witness statement from Esme Shepherd – I've no reason to doubt it and it can probably be verified by Eunice Villiers, providing she's well enough to do so.'
'What did she say?'
'Well, you'll find this incredible I think, Sir.'
Boase drew up a chair and proceeded to tell Superintendent Bolton everything that had been said the previous day.

'So, are you actually telling me that she ended the pregnancy of Eunice Villiers and that he actually forced it on her?'

'Yes – that's how it seems, Sir.'

That's terrible. So – in revenge, he set about ruining Esme Shepherd by attacking her customers – why didn't he just tell us she was performing acts that were against the law of the land?'

'I suppose then, if he did that, there was a chance that he would be revealed as someone who had availed himself on behalf of his wife?'

'Well, maybe – but it's a bit drastic to take his murderous ways out on the woman's innocent customers.'

'I know, Sir.'

Boase looked thoughtful for a moment.

'Oh, Boase – look, I'm sorry, I keep forgetting how close to all this you are, with Irene and everything, forgive me, I was thoughtless.'

'That's okay, Sir.'

But, Boase - I still don't know how we're going to make this stick to him.'

'Let's hope when he realises, he'll confess. He's covered his tracks successfully all along. But we know he sold the poisoned foods, we know he had the expertise to make the stuff – and people have identified him as being the commercial traveller. It's no coincidence that only three establishments in the whole of Falmouth were targeted – and all three were co-owned by Esme Shepherd. I just feel sorry for her partners in business, they didn't do anything to deserve that. Unless they've very careful now, all three will be ruined for good.'

'I know, that's dreadful bad luck – but maybe, when all this business is over, they'll bounce back. What's your plan now? Go over to see Villiers?'

'Yes, I think I should – assuming he went home last night?'

'I should imagine he did, go over there and talk to him again, use what you know wisely. 'Want me to come?'

'No thank you, Sir – but I might take Coad with me…just in case there's any trouble.'

'Well, bring him in – on anything you can, don't forget the attack on that Pellow girl if necessary.'

'Will do, Sir.'

'Coad – you're coming with me this morning, out to see Villiers and the plan is to bring him back here. We think he probably went home last night after being discharged from the hospital, let's hope he's there when we arrive. I wouldn't put it past him to run off, he knows we're on to him. Come on – let's get there as quickly as we can.'

As the car reached the top of Killigrew, arriving at the recreation ground, Boase grabbed Coad's arm.

'Stop the car!'

The car swerved and mounted the pavement slightly.

'You frightened the life out of me, shouting like that.'

Boase was already out of the car and running up the road.

'Irene, Irene. Stand still. I'm coming.'

Irene Bartlett was standing on the kerb looking bewildered amongst the noise of the traffic.

'Archie – is that you, oh, thank heaven. Please help me.'

As Boase reached her, he thought how small and vulnerable she looked standing on the edge of the pavement with her white cane.

'Irene, what are you doing out here on your own?'

'Well, I've been trying to get used to using this stick – I've been out once or twice on my own but only to the top of Penmere. Today I thought I'd go a bit further. I managed to cross the road but then I felt a little confused and I just panicked and froze.'

'It's all right, sweetheart – I'm here now. Here – take my arm. It's a good job I saw you. Look, walk over here with me, the car is just there, I'll take you home.'

'Thank you, Archie – I got so frightened and I didn't know what to do. Please don't tell Mum and Dad, they really don't like me going out alone.'

'I won't say a word, I'll just say I stopped to give you a lift.'

'Thank you so much, Archie.'

The couple had reached the car which Coad had managed to reverse back off the pavement. Boase put Irene in the back and sat in beside her.

'Just drive down to Penmere a minute, will you, Coad?'

The car drew up outside the Bartlett house and Boase helped Irene out of the car and up to the front door.'

'Just go in, Archie, it'll be open.'

Boase opened the front door and let Irene inside. Topper came bouncing through the hall, wagging his tail.

'All right, boy – let me get in.'

'Everything okay, Irene?'

Caroline Bartlett came through into the hall, followed by her husband.

'Yes, Mrs Bartlett, I just saw Irene at the top of the road on her way back so I thought I'd give her a lift.'

'Thank you, Archie – I don't like her going out alone.'

'It's fine, Mum, really, don't fuss. Thank you for the lift, Archie. I was feeling a bit tired.'

'You staying for a cup of tea, my boy?'

'No thanks, Sir – I've got Coad waiting for me…we've got a criminal to catch.'

'Sounds interesting…who you after?'

Before Bartlett could get a reply, Boase had kissed Irene on the cheek and run out through the front door to the waiting car.

Chapter Nineteen

'I've got a bad feeling that our man is going to make a run for it, Coad – drive as quickly as you can.'

'Surely if he wanted to get away, he'd have gone last night? And where would he go?'

'He's got pots of money – he could go anywhere he wanted I should think.'

As the car negotiated the narrow lanes and bends down towards the Helford River, Coad suddenly pressed hard on the brakes as he came round a corner almost driving straight into a herd of cows in the middle of the road.

'Oh no!'

Boase leaned out of the window and called out to the farmer.

'Are you going to be much longer with this lot? I'm on urgent police business!'

The farmer grinned, showing one large brown tooth in the centre of that grin.

'Well, the bleddy cows don't know you from Adam – you go upsetting them and their milk will curdle.'

'Just hurry up, would you please?'

'You're just making him go slower.'

Coad was tapping on the steering wheel.

'Can you stop that please, you're just making things worse.'

'Sorry.'

The cows eventually entered one by one into a field and the farmer, closing the five-bar gate behind him, leaned on it and waved as the car drove past.

'Blasted man.'

'It's all right, I'm just about to turn into Villiers' road – don't panic.'

As the car rounded the bend approaching Villiers' house, Coad swerved into the hedge.'

'What on earth?'

Boase turned around just in time to see the back of Edgar Villiers' sports motor car driving off into the distance in the opposite direction.

'He's gone – if it wasn't for that blasted farmer, we'd have been in time.'

Coad was already out of the car, assessing the damage.

'We're in a ditch – I didn't have any choice, he would have hit us head on.'

'I know – you did well. How are we going to get out of here?'

As the two men tried to lift the front end of the car, the farmer came walking towards them. Boase looked up.

'Oh, Lord – what does he want now?'

Coad saw the man approaching.

'Come to gloat I expect – but he is carrying a shovel.'

The farmer never spoke as he pushed the large shovel down into the ditch, giving Boase and Coad the leverage they needed to free the car. Now Boase had to thank him. Coad intervened.

'Leave this to me – I know it'll be too painful for you.'

'I'm sorry about just now – we were in a terrible hurry and very late.'

As the farmer walked past Boase he muttered.

'Bit later now you are.'

And he was gone.

212

The car removed from the ditch, Coad drove the car back to Falmouth. When they arrived they sat outside the station for a moment. Boase thought about what just happened.

'Where do you think he was going, Coad?'

'I have no idea – and as you say, with all his money, he could go anywhere. Probably has lots of rich friends abroad too.'

'Oh, don't say that – if he leaves the country, we've had it.'

Boase stared through the windscreen.

'But I know if I was he and running away, there'd be one or two things I'd do first. Start the car up.'

'Where are we going?'

'Do you remember where Topsy Beaufort's grave is?'

'Well, I've never been, but Penhaligon told me just where it was because he saw Villiers there before.'

'Precisely, that's where I'm hoping he's gone now. Just to say goodbye. Come on – quickly.'

The car reached the cemetery and the two men got out and walked over to the grave. No one was around.

'Well, I expected to see him here, Coad.'

Coad bent down to the grave.

'There are some fresh violets here, look. Maybe he just brought them then left?'

'Well, that's a let-down. But…'

'…but what?'

'There is possibly one more place we could try.'

Eunice Villiers stood up at the window, waving and tapping on the glass.

'What on earth are you doing, Mrs Villiers? Come on now, sit down.'

The young nurse who had just come on duty walked over to the window to help the woman back to her chair. As they both looked out, they could see Edgar Villiers walking across the gardens from his car. He stopped, lit a cigarette and looked up at his wife's window. He waved back to her. She looked at the nurse and beamed, probably for the first time since they had known her at Meadowbank. A moment later he was in the room. He hugged his wife then he addressed the nurse.

'Look, I'd like to speak to my wife privately if that's all right. I'm aware you feel that I've been neglecting her of late and, well, that's probably true. But as you all know here, I'm in business and I'm a very busy man – that's how I manage to pay your wages. The young nurse giggled and offered to bring some tea.

'Eunice, my darling, I'm so sorry for all the hurt I've caused you – you know I love you dear, don't you?'

Eunice nodded and reached for her husband's hand.

'I'm sorry for everything I've done and I truly want to make it up to you. Can you ever forgive me, Eunice, my love?'

Eunice squeezed his hand.

'Oh look, my dear, here's that lovely young nurse with some tea for us. Shall I be mother?'

'Can't this thing go any faster, Coad? Shall I drive?'

'It won't make any difference, we've done top speed since Falmouth.'

'Well – no need to be so careless either – you almost knocked that man off his motorcycle.'

The car turned into the drive way passing the sign at the entrance bearing the legend 'Meadowbank Home for the Insane.'

Boase tutted.

'Don't know how they get away with that – drawing attention to sick people like that. It could come to any one of us, at any moment, Coad. They don't know why these people aren't in their right mind, what they've been through – what they've seen.'

Coad was prepared to take Boase's word for that as he stopped the car outside the large house. He pointed to the corner of the garden.

'He's here – look that's his car.'

'Right – let's hope he hasn't seen us. Just follow me.'

Boase and Coad entered the imposing lobby. No one was around. Boase whispered.

'Looks like these are all offices – guess the rooms are upstairs.'

The two ascended the ornate staircase and, on reaching the top, met with the young nurse looking after Mrs Villiers. Boase went across to her desk.

'Excuse me nurse, we're the police. Is Mr Villiers here?'

'Yes, he's been here about twenty minutes – he's visiting his wife.'

'I'm sorry to ask, but it's important that I interrupt their meeting.'

'Oh, well, I don't think Matron would like you to do that.'

'Is Matron here?'

'Well... no.'

'Then, if you don't tell her, neither will I. Which is Mrs Villiers' room?'

The nurse indicated in the direction of the room. Boase and Coad went across to the door.

'Right, Coad – when we go in, don't let him get past you. Ready?'

Coad nodded and Boase tried the door. It wouldn't open. He tried again and the door moved slightly.

'He's put a chair under it.'

The young nurse was watching what was happening. She went across to Boase and spoke in a low voice. There's another door to that room straight from Matron's office.'

'Oh – thank you. Take us to Matron's office.'

In this room, they went across to the door linking the rooms. Boase pushed open the door an inch. He could see the Villiers couple through the crack. He listened for a moment.

'Come on, Eunice, dear – drink this lovely tea.'

Eunice shook her head.

'Drink the blasted stuff. For pity's sake woman. Look, I'm having mine, it's perfectly safe.'

At that, Boase burst through the adjoining door, followed by Coad.

'Stop there, Villiers.'

The man looked up and, like a whippet, sprung to the other door, pulled the chair away and, throwing it into Boase's path, ran down the stairs.'

'Boase – he's getting away.'

With seemingly super-stamina the man out-ran Boase and to his car which was the nearer. Jumping inside, he started the motor and sped off down the drive. Boase and Coad raced to their car and sped off down the drive after Villiers.

'He's gone – I can't keep up.'

'Just drive, Coad. We can't let him get away.'

They continued on for about a mile.

'I don't know which way he went.'

'Stop! Reverse the car.'

They had just passed a small turning on the left hand side and Boase had glanced out of his window. He saw Villiers' car disappearing down the lane.

'Just saw him – he went down there.'

Coad reversed the car and drove down the lane.

'You sure this is right?'

'Yes – I saw him just disappearing round this bend.'

'All that's down here is Gwennap Pit. Why would he go there?'

'He's probably panicking – trying to hide. He doesn't think we'll find him. He's probably planning to stay here until it gets dark, then he'll be on his way.'

They continued on towards Gwennap Pit, an open-air amphitheatre; the strange circular feature had been turfed and was regularly used for preaching the Methodist faith.

'Stop here, Coad. Why has he come here – look there's his car outside the pit.'

The two policemen got out of the car and walked to Villiers' car. Boase peered inside. There were two suitcases on the back seat.

'He was going somewhere – but he's not now. He must have gone into the pit. Come on, Coad. The two men carefully and quietly went up to the amphitheatre.

'You go that side, I'll go this. Don't let him see you. Keep this entrance covered too. Don't let him get past you.'

Coad nudged Boase's arm.

'Look, he's walking down into the pit.'

They watched as Villiers walked halfway down the green-stepped amphitheatre. It had been raining lightly and the ground was muddy. As they watched, Villiers suddenly sank to his knees. He clutched his head with both hands and fell completely, tumbling uncontrollably towards the centre of the pit. Boase and Coad ran down after him as quickly as they could. When they reached him, he was face down. Boase turned him over.

'Is he dead?'

'No – but look at him, he's salivating profusely...and look at this rash appearing on his cheeks.'

'What do you think has happened to him?'

'I'm not sure, Coad – but we need to get him to hospital.'

'How are we going to carry him all the way back up there? He's huge!'

'Don't start – we can't leave him here. We'll just have to do our best. There's no one else here.'

The two men lifted Villiers between them and carried him back up to the top, stopping on every other step. Coad was breathing heavily and rapidly by the time they reached the top.

'How are you so unfit, Coad? You've got to be seven or eight years younger than me.'

'I think I'm probably dead right now.'

'Stop moaning, open his car door – I'll drive it back and put it round the back of the station to keep it safe.'

'Why can't I drive the sports car?'

'Because I'm in charge. You follow me, if I stop, it's because he's taken a turn for the worse. He's still breathing at the moment but he's not looking good.'

The two cars raced back to Falmouth, Coad barely able to keep up with Boase. They arrived at the hospital and carried the man in. The doctor admitting him asked them to wait while he checked him over. The two sat in the lobby. Coad leaned across to Boase and whispered.

'What do you think is wrong with him?'

'I have no idea and I'm not a gambling man – but it looks to me like poison.'

'Really – why would he do that to himself?'

'Maybe he realised the game was up and he was well and truly caught.'

'I can't imagine someone like that would do that.'

'You never know what's going on in someone's mind, Coad.'

The doctor returned to speak to them.

'Constable, this must be off the record until we've done tests, but we've learned enough of these symptoms over the last little while to make a reasonable diagnosis at this stage.'

'Go on.'

'Thallium.'
'Again? Thank you, very much, doctor. Please keep the station updated?'
'Of course.'
Boase and Coad returned to the cars.
'Well, Coad, there you are. He used his expert and prize-winning knowledge of thallium to try to kill himself. What do you make of that?'
'Be interesting to see if he pulls through.'

The sports car parked safely in the police garage for the night, Boase arranged with Meadowbank to visit Mrs Villiers the next morning and then left to go home. He took a short detour to the Bartlett's house – to tell Bartlett of the latest developments, and, of course, to see Irene. He didn't stay long, he was tired and it had seemed rather a long day. Bartlett was startled by what Boase had to tell him, announcing that he really hadn't expected this outcome.

By half past eight the next morning, Boase was travelling alone to see Eunice Villiers. She was in her room with the young nurse who had been with her the previous day.
'Don't make her too tired, will you, Constable?'
'No, don't worry, I won't keep her long. I'd like to speak to you too, if you don't mind.'
'No – that's okay. Did you catch that horrible man?'
Boase stared at her.
'What makes you say he's a horrible man?'
'I'll let Mrs Villiers tell you herself.'
'But – can she...I mean...?'
'Yes – after her husband's visit yesterday, we've seen a change in her. Her speech isn't very good but she's happy to talk to you.'
'That's excellent news, thank you.'

Boase and the nurse sat with Mrs Villiers.

'Was there something you wanted to tell me, Mrs Villiers?'

'Yes. Want to tell you.'

The woman's voice was slurred but this was probably the first time she had made anything other than unintelligible sounds since she had been here.

'In your own time, please.'

'He wanted to kill me.'

'Who wanted to kill you, Mrs Villiers?'

'Edgar.'

'Why would he want to do that to you?'

The woman stopped speaking and stared into the distance. The nurse patted her hand.

'It's all right, Eunice, you're doing so well.'

'Yes, you really are.'

Boase didn't want the woman to stop talking.

The nurse addressed him from behind Mrs Villiers' chair.'

Her speech is slow but I think her mind has always been sharp.'

'Yes, my mind has always been sharp.'

Boase grinned at the nurse.

'He killed my baby.'

'Can you tell me what happened?'

'He killed my baby because it wasn't his. He made a woman come and take my baby away.'

The young nurse looked horrified to hear this.

'The he brought me here.'

Mrs Villiers looked at Boase.

'I didn't want to live without my baby, my only baby, so he brought me here. He didn't want the trouble of me being ill.'

A tear fell from the woman's eye.

'It's all right, Mrs, Villiers, you don't need to talk about that anymore.'

'No…listen. He put poison in my tea yesterday.'

Boase looked at her, watching her face.

'How do you know – and why would he do that?'

Because I saw him do it and because he's been mean all his life. He didn't want to keep paying for me to live in here because he's mean. My father used to say he only wanted me for my money but I didn't want to believe that, but, it was true. He took all my money for his silly little experiments. Yes, he came from a wealthy family – but mine was wealthier.'

'So what happened with the poison yesterday?'

'I switched the cups when he wasn't looking. He just thought I was a stupid, sick woman. But I expected it. He could see how much I was costing him and he didn't want the expense any more. I used to be very clever, young man.'

'I think you still are. You outwitted him.'

'Yes, I think I probably did. I hope he drank it all before he left.'

'Yes, I think he did – I'm afraid he's in hospital now.'

'Good job. I'm tired now. Nurse, I think I'd like to lie down for a little while.'

Boase stood up.

'Thank you so much, Mrs Villiers – and I wish you a speedy recovery; you're seeming better already.'

Boase travelled back to Falmouth, his head spinning with so much information. Good old Mrs Villiers – she was very smart, and she hadn't let her husband beat her. He felt a little hungry so he called in to the baker's shop and bought himself a rather large cream cake to have with his cup of tea later. He went into the police station where he was stopped by the desk sergeant.

'Superintendent Bolton asked me to send you in to see him when you arrived.'

'Oh – well, let me put my cake safely in my desk drawer and I'll go up.'

Boase sat in the Superintendent's office.

'I've just had a message from the hospital about an hour ago – Edgar Villiers is dead.'

'Dead? Oh my word.'

'Yes – looks like he killed himself.'

'Who told you that, Sir?'

'Well, what else could it have been – I expect he knew the game was up and that we were on to him, it was only a matter of time before we arrested him.'

'I'm sorry to say, that's not correct, Sir.'

'What do you mean?'

'Well, the last time I saw you, Sir, was when I was getting ready to see Villiers. Well, one unexpected thing led to another – it's all in my notes, Sir, up until this morning, that is. So I have a lot to tell you.'

'Pull up a chair.'

Boase sat down, longing for the cream cake he had purchased.

'Sir, Edgar Villiers didn't kill himself, well not exactly – no, he was planning to run away but not before he'd done away with Mrs Villiers.'

'*What?*'

'It's true, Sir – he went to Meadowbank yesterday. Coad and I caught up with him – he had gone there to poison his wife?'

'Why would he do a fool thing like that?'

'That's what I've just asked Mrs Villiers this morning; I've just come back from there again. She said he was so mean that if she was dead, he wouldn't have to keep paying her fees.'

'Well I never. Anything else?'

'Yes, plenty, Sir.'

Boase sat with Bolton for over an hour telling him what had happened and the conclusions he'd arrived at.

'Well, I have to say, Boase, you're a remarkable young man – you've done an excellent job and with not much help I have to say. I haven't been much use to you either and I'm sorry about that.'

Boase wasn't going to argue about that one. Yes – he had done it on his own but he couldn't have done it without the help of a very clever man, George Bartlett – he had listened to Boase and offered him advice and guidance. Boase couldn't have got through without him.

Boase made another attempt to return to his cream cake.

'Oh – just one other thing, I hope I'm not talking out of turn and that you will be utterly discreet. There's talk of George Bartlett being asked to return.'

'Inspector Bartlett – coming back?'

'Well, we don't know but I've got a feeling it's on the cards...that he'll be asked, that is. And you didn't hear anything from me – understand?'

'Yes, absolutely understand, Sir. Thank you, Sir.'

Boase walked back to his office as though he hadn't a care in the world. What a weight off his mind this was. He hoped Bartlett would say yes; of course he would. He may already have been asked. He wondered when Bartlett would tell him – but of course he would have to wait until he said something, he couldn't, mustn't, let anyone know that this was happening. Boase looked at the cake and, forgetting all about the tea, ate it as though he hadn't eaten for a week.

A hand written note had appeared on the sergeant's desk – it was on lilac scented paper. As Boase walked by, the sergeant passed it to him.

'This was brought in for you, about half an hour ago.'

'Thanks.'

Sitting at his desk, Boase looked at the familiar paper. He held it up to his nostrils and smiled. Carefully, using his paper knife, he cut open the paper and read the contents. It was in Caroline Bartlett's handwriting – an invitation to supper that same evening at seven o'clock. At the bottom, and almost slipping off the corner of the page was one word *Irene.'* Boase felt so touched – Irene had actually managed to sign her name, for him. It was scrawled and irregular but he still recognised the hand as hers.

And so it was that Boase arrived for supper at the Bartlett house. As the four of them sat and ate and Boase and Irene held hands under the table, Bartlett tapped his beer glass with his spoon, and rose from the table.

'Ladies and gentleman – oh, and of course, Topper.'

Topper sat bolt upright at the mention of his name and took the piece of ham that Boase has smuggled under the table. Bartlett coughed theatrically.

'I have an important announcement to make which may come as a surprise to all of you. I have today received this communication through the post from my, shall I say, previous employer? In this missive it appears that they have looked at all aspects of previous events and they have asked if I would consider returning to my previous situation.

'Dad! That's wonderful news –are you going back?'

'Congratulations, Sir – excellent.'

Caroline Bartlett remained silent.

'Well, Princess – haven't you got anything to say?'

'That's marvellous news, George, dear, it really is.'

'What's wrong – aren't you pleased?'

'Of course I am, I know how much you've missed being there.'

'Well why the glum face then?'

'It's fine dear, I've just got used to having you around, that's all – and it's been lovely…you go ahead. I'm very pleased for you, dear.'

'Well, look now – I don't have to decide straight away. This is what I'm going to do.'

Bartlett stood up and replacing the letter in its envelope, pushed it behind the clock on the mantelpiece.

'Let's forget all about it for a day or two and then, well, then I'll have another think. In the meantime, I think I would like to propose a toast to an excellent policeman. I hear that you had a good result with your cases, Boase. Well done, very well done indeed.'

Bartlett raised his beer glass in the air.

'To Boase.'

Irene giggled as she and her mother raised their teacups.

'To Boase.'

Irene squeezed Boase's hand tightly.

'Well done, Archie, very well done. I'm so proud of you. Let's hope your next case will be with Dad.'

'Oh, I hope so, Irene – I do hope so.'

Lightning Source UK Ltd.
Milton Keynes UK
UKHW05f2332120718
325550UK00019B/791/P